Jolan
away

But the grip on her wrist tightened and she glanced up into Vito's menacing eyes.

"Damn you, Vito Velardi!" she whispered. "Damn you for resurrecting everything I want to forget!"

"Face it," he growled. "Remember. Remember how it was. The fear. The screams, the dust, the pressure on your lungs, the pain in your head." He shook her roughly. "You have to do it, Jolanda."

For a brief moment she recalled the sensation of being unable to breathe, and her frightened gaze was held by his piercing, blazing eyes.

"You remember something," he muttered. "Think, Jolanda!"

"No," she moaned, her head tipping back to avoid being mesmerized. Then she shivered in shock.

SARA WOOD lives in a rambling sixteenth-century home in the medieval town of Lewes amid the Sussex hills. Her sons have claimed the cellar for bikes, making ferret cages, taxidermy and winemaking, while Sara has virtually taken over the study with her reference books, word processor and what have you. Her amiable, tolerant husband, she says, squeezes in wherever he finds room. After having tried many careers—secretary, guest house proprietor, play-group owner and primary teacher—she now finds writing romance novels gives her enormous pleasure.

Books by Sara Wood

HARLEQUIN PRESENTS
1166—THE COUNT'S VENDETTA
1182—TENDER PERSUASION
1206—NO GENTLE LOVING
1302—THREAT OF POSSESSION
1318—LOVE NOT DISHONOUR
1382—NIGHTS OF DESTINY
1414—DESERT HOSTAGE

HARLEQUIN ROMANCE
2814—PERFUMES OF ARABIA
3066—MASTER OF CASHEL

Don't miss any of our special offers. Write to us at the following address for information on our newest releases.

Harlequin Reader Service
P.O. Box 1397, Buffalo, NY 14240
Canadian address: P.O. Box 603,
Fort Erie, Ont. L2A 5X3

SARA WOOD

sicilian vengeance

Harlequin Books

TORONTO • NEW YORK • LONDON
AMSTERDAM • PARIS • SYDNEY • HAMBURG
STOCKHOLM • ATHENS • TOKYO • MILAN
MADRID • WARSAW • BUDAPEST • AUCKLAND

Harlequin Presents first edition June 1992
ISBN 0-373-11470-2

Original hardcover edition published in 1990
by Mills & Boon Limited

SICILIAN VENGEANCE

All the characters in this book have no existence outside the
imagination of the author and have no relation whatsoever to
anyone bearing the same name or names. They are not even
distantly inspired by any individual known or unknown to the
author, and all incidents are pure invention.

® are Trademarks registered in the United States Patent and
Trademark Office and in other countries.

Printed in U.S.A.

CHAPTER ONE

VITO'S face was guarded, as usual, his dark eyes non-committal as he gazed down on Nick, who was lying in bed, his face creased with pain.

'Jolanda will never come,' said Vito flatly.

Nick made a helpless gesture with his shoulders and winced, prompting his wife Angela to plump up his pillows.

'I want Jolanda here!' said Nick stubbornly. 'I want my twin. Oh, how could you understand, Vito? You're so self-sufficient; you need no one. That's why we all flock around you, I suppose.'

'Like gulls around refuse?' mocked Vito.

'Why are you always putting yourself down?' frowned Nick.

'Someone has to,' said Vito laconically, reaching for his sunglasses. 'Well, if that's all——'

'No, dammit!' cried Nick impatiently. 'I won't be side-tracked. Will you bring her to Sicily or not?'

'I hardly imagine she'll thank me for doing so,' drawled Vito. 'She's had plenty of opportunity to visit over the past years. Somehow I doubt that she's breathlessly panting with the desire to tread the hallowed soil of a remote hilltop town.'

Nick flushed. 'She just doesn't know what it's like here—— '

'You can say that again.' Vito's mouth looked more haughty than usual. 'She'd get the shock of her little life if she had to manage without a manicurist and pre-packed meals close to hand.'

'You're wrong. I adapted, after an equally comfortable life. We had the same background, you, me, and Jolanda. If you and I can live in Rocca, why can't she? I need to see her. Being a twin is different from any other relationship. She's part of me.'

Vito eyed Nick thoughtfully, his eyes bleak. 'You two were never close.'

'Please!' Nick looked upset. 'We've been through all that. You owe me a favour. You'll soon have control of the company; that's what you want; it's what I want too. And now, in return, you can help me to make peace with my sister.'

'You'll regret it,' Vito said harshly. 'She's not cut out for the simple life.'

'She'll love Rocca, once she gets to know her way around. And she's never even met Angela.'

Nick smiled lovingly on his golden-haired wife. Vito shook his head in disagreement.

'Love it? A city girl? Don't fool yourself. She won't adore rough country pasta, inadequate water supplies and the simple entertainments an isolated village can provide. She's used to partying around, dressing up, being admired. There would be precious little of that here.'

But Nick was certain that his twin would share his affection for his home. Particularly if Vito was a frequent visitor. Didn't she hero-worship Vito as he did, as everyone did?

'You're a pessimist,' said Nick ruefully.

'Close, but not entirely accurate,' corrected Vito. 'No true Sicilian pins his faith on anything, particularly the decisions of women. And, from what I know of Jolanda, she likes change and excitement. The stark and tedious realities of peasant life would go down like a ton of bricks on a builder's toe.'

'Don't underestimate her. When she knows the problems here, she'll want to stay.'

Vito gave Nick a wintry smile. 'Not everyone is as noble as you. You're asking a lot of your sister, to give up a good job and a way of life she evidently adores, to live and work in a strange country.'

'Leave that part to me. This is a favour I'm after from you, my friend, my adopted brother,' urged Nick. 'Persuade her. Tell her, at least, that I'm ill and would like to see her, if only for a brief visit. Can you refuse me?'

Vito frowned on the pain-racked figure of Nick, lying between the cool white sheets. Nick ought to let well alone. This hare-brained idea of his was a mistake. It would be like transplanting an orchid into a bed of rotting cabbage. With an inner sigh, Vito realised that he should have seen this coming. Nick had been blinded by family values ever since he'd married the gentle Angela.

'Last time——' he began.

'Last time we three were together, we were all unable to keep our tempers. It'll be different now. Vito! Remember the fun we had, as kids?'

'No,' he growled, his eyes glittering like wet coals. 'It was fun for you, deadly serious for me.'

He stopped Nick's retort with a furious glare. Trying to bring back the rose-coloured illusion of childhood companionship was futile. For a start, that had never existed, only in Nick's mind. The action Nick planned would bring him nothing but heartache. The flirtatious, desperate to please Jolanda had become flighty and shallow. A user of men. A mercenary, cold-hearted bitch.

It would be better for Nick to hold on to that fantasy of a devoted, sweet-natured sister than have his fancies shattered.

'Please,' begged Angela, her eyes tender with concern for her husband. 'Part of Nick's pain is caused by the separation from his twin. You of all people know what grief is; you understand what it is to be parted from loved ones. Look how it affected you.'

He winced, even though her words were softened by her sympathetic expression. 'Unfair tactics, Angela,' he murmured, a faint rasp in his voice betraying the searing pain inside him.

'But effective, I think,' she answered serenely. She and Vito understood one another.

He nodded. She, too, was Sicilian, and therefore used any means to reach her objective. It was time he went, before she dug any deeper and struck more raw nerves.

'Be it on your own heads,' he sighed, capitulating and kissing Angela on both cheeks. He bent to clasp Nick's hot hand and embrace him, Sicilian style. 'I'll get her over here,' he promised. 'But it'll take some persuasion to do so.'

'I know.' Nick's lines of anguish eased out with the happy smile. 'I'd rather she thought it was her own idea. You can arrange that, can't you? Be devious, Vito; you're a past master at that!'

Vito grinned and waved farewell. Nick had no idea just how devious he intended to be. His mind already buzzed with complicated plans. Jolanda would have to be slotted into them.

A faint smile lit his eyes. She shouldn't be too difficult to coax. If she was as fun-loving as her reputation gave her credit for, well, he had enough amusements for a full-scale funfair. He'd give her a roller-coaster ride she'd never forget and whisk her off to her brother before she could draw breath.

It might even be diverting.

He wedged his sunglasses firmly on his aristocratic nose and pulled down the brim of the expensive straw hat he'd bought in Milan; a lithe and beautiful man, aware of the murmuring women in the doorways, the stony-faced old men sitting beneath the plane trees in the shade, talking about him as they always did, discussing his life as if it belonged to them.

As he walked along the narrow alleys and down the rough stepped streets to his car which he'd had to park in the tiny piazza, he tried to look at the village through Jolanda's eyes.

Noon struck. For half an hour there was bedlam as everyone in the village headed for home in bone-shaking cars or misfiring motorscooters, on the back of a skinny horse or on their own two feet. Vito drew a cigar from his breast pocket and watched the traffic jams, the shouting, the chaos. Suddenly the alleys were deserted. All sound ceased. Not a typewriter clacking, a child laughing, a bell ringing.

Oh, yes, he thought with certainty. She'd hate it: the damp peeling walls, the grey cobbles, the rusting balconies. She'd loathe the isolation, the fact that she couldn't easily obtain the luxuries of life which had become necessities. She'd be appalled that a large section of the village was still *abandonati*, declared unsafe over twenty-two years ago. The day they'd all met, so violently. He scowled at the irony of Fate.

Jolanda must slip in, and out of his life again. She must be persuaded to sell him her half of the construction company, but she must not like Sicily. It was important that she saw all its faults. If she missed any

of these things, he, Vito Velardi, would point them out
to her. He had a few old scores to settle and she had
unwittingly become involved in his plans.

Vito's dark eyes gleamed with satisfaction and his lean
hands clenched as if preparing for a fight. But his assault wouldn't be physical. He was far too subtle for any
crude approach. An English upbringing and education
had neither dampened the fire in his blood, nor tem-
pered the natural mistrust of his people. He'd spent his
youth fighting against blunt English values.

Poor Jolanda. Her schoolbook cleverness was no
defence against his native wit.

'... So there I was in this beach-tent affair, wearing just
a suntan, and this huge hairy hand slid through the
opening.' Jolanda took a quick sip of her Hawaiian
sunset cocktail, and resumed. 'I grabbed my Filofax and
bashed away at the hand; the man fell on to the tent and
it collapsed on top of us. I crawled out starkers, my
precious Filofax safely in my hand with this thief floun-
dering in a mass of guy ropes, to see everyone on the
beach and my father absolutely *riveted*.'

Her audience, equally riveted, laughed in delight and
waited for the inevitable punch line.

'What did he say?' grinned Charlotte, since Jolanda
seemed to be waiting for someone to ask.

'He said, "A novel way to do business, Jolanda," and
calmly strolled away!'

Her infectious laughter rang out and was drowned by
the noise of the party. Despite an annoying, dull ache
in the upper part of her spine, Jolanda was enjoying
herself. She was with her friends and Max, who was
standing adoringly by her side. The party he was giving

on board a river steamer, moored to a Thames jetty, looked like being fun.

'Anyway,' she added, 'I sold more property that week in Cannes than we actually possessed. We had to do a bit of impromptu buying ourselves. Father asked if I'd stage my little exhibition right along the French Riviera. Said we'd make a fortune.'

She raised her dark, expressive eyes to heaven at the thought and her friends roared. The women knew that Jolanda was beautiful enough to be able to tell stories against herself and their laughter was tinged with envy.

Jolanda was stunning, vivacious and funny. Tonight, impeccably made up, with her long black hair artfully tumbled to frame her face, and in a cotton velvet sheath which acted like a second skin, she was particularly eye-catching.

But she treated everyone alike, men and women, rich and poor. Outwardly friendly and extrovert, she never poached another woman's boyfriend, however willing they might be. And for that the women were grateful. She could have been dangerous, otherwise. Odd, how sexy she looked: as if she had a secret lover and was cheating on Max. Perhaps she had. The gossip flowed, as usual.

'Your father is a very laid-back man,' sighed Charlotte.

'Heavens! I'm twenty-five and lead my own life. He gave up beating me long ago,' grinned Jolanda.

'That was obviously a mistake,' said a slow, drawling voice behind her. It oozed over her shoulder like golden honey laced with whisky.

Jolanda whirled around in shock, her beautiful face briefly vulnerable, her black mane of hair flying in all directions. And then she recovered herself and became the bright, sparkling sophisticate again.

'Vito!' she cried warmly. Her red lips shaped into a slightly wicked smile. 'Did you find a hacksaw in your prison porridge? Or are you out on parole? I never thought Immigration would let you into the country again!'

Vito's cynical eyes took her all in, slowly, deliberately, and with utter contempt. He made no attempt to deny her wild accusation and she wondered why. *Had* one of his borderline escapades resulted in a prison sentence, as she'd suggested? You never knew with Vito. He had always lived on the edge of danger.

'Money oiled a few reluctant wheels,' he said laconically, leaving her guessing. The guests perked up at the prospect of a novel entertainment. 'My fists oiled the rest.'

'Oh. Corruption and violence. Just your style.'

His eyes were mocking, in response to the *frisson* which had run around the group. He swept a sardonic glance over them all and then his dark, compelling gaze returned to Jolanda.

'Isn't it just?'

'So you have been in prison,' she persisted.

'As a matter of fact, I have,' he said. 'I had enough cash and energy left over to catch a bus so that I could sample the party of the year. This *is* it, isn't it?' he asked, peering around as if he didn't think much of the action.

Jolanda angled her head to one side. 'You're a liar. You've never ridden on a bus in your whole life. And I bet you've been catching up on your embroidery since I saw you last.'

'I'm always embroidering. I never stop.'

Her eyes hardened. Vito was incapable of straight-talking. His conversation was peppered with lies. Yes, he embroidered.

'Where's your invitation?' she demanded. 'I didn't know Max had invited any snake-charmers to his shindig.'

Vito merely stared her down, a supercilious dislike deepening the lines running down to his Romeo mouth.

Jolanda tried not to be mesmerised by it. She could feel the tension building between them, as it always had.

'I didn't ask him,' frowned Max. 'Who is this?'

Vito lifted one eyebrow at her and managed to look sultry.

'This?' She paused, giving herself time to flick a bored glance up and down his elegant body. 'Vito Velardi,' she said lightly, her heart beating fast. Damn the man, he knocked spots off anyone in the room! What was it about Italian men that gave them so much enviable style and tantalising hints of passionate intensity? 'He's a wraith from my past, darling.'

'Some wraith!' enthused Charlotte, eyeing the well-built Vito with greedy eyes and pushing out her chest in his direction.

'Yes,' said Jolanda sharply. 'Popped up from Hell. Bedfellow of Dracula. He haunts women, sinks his fangs into them and then slips from their grasp like a ghost. If you value your mortality, Charlotte, fend him off with a string of garlic. Preferably by tying it tightly around his neck.'

'I think your metaphors got a little mixed up there, Jolanda.'

As Vito murmured that, his gaze was slowly and enjoyably touring Charlotte's low-cut, thigh-high dress, leaving its occupant quivering from the sexual menace he injected into his expression.

'It's amazing what a clever designer can do with a hatband and some tiny frills, isn't it?' he marvelled.

Without drawing breath, he turned back to Max. 'Jolanda and I were very close. We slept together. Fancy you not hearing about that.'

Max stared at her aghast and she bristled. What was Vito up to? Already he'd disconcerted them all. It was a knack he had. Charlotte's blue eyes were fluttering alarmingly. She was intrigued by his casual air of self-containment and calm, deliberate movements. Jolanda had seen his style at parties before. He stood to one side, assessing who was worth his time, and in the process he drew women as a magnet attracted iron filings. And he was lethal.

'My God! You lived with this man?' asked Max in a strangled voice.

Jolanda felt the press of the crowd around her. Everyone would be fascinated to know more about the handsome gate-crasher.

'Unfortunately. I was three years old at the time. Father adopted him,' she said grudgingly. 'There was nothing sexual about our relationship. We were like brother and sister.'

'Yes,' provided Vito, his dark eyes thoughtful. 'We fought like cat and dog.'

'Oh!' Max let out his breath in relief. 'I thought he meant...' He laughed. 'That was stupid of me. I should have known you better. I'm sorry.'

'Yes,' she said sourly, knowing why he was kicking himself for even briefly imagining she might harbour passion. Max was one of the few men who knew her. Jolanda Docherty never got involved in anything earnest unless it was business. 'Stupid,' she agreed, with a toss of her head.

'You never told me about him, darling,' said Max, his voice a little complaining and reproachful.

Jolanda shrugged her slender tanned shoulders. 'There was nothing interesting to tell.'

'Did it all mean so little to you, Jolanda?' murmured Vito suggestively.

She felt her face colouring up. Max's eyes ran suspiciously up and down Vito's arrogant body.

'This adopted brother bit... He doesn't share your surname, darling.'

Max had staked his claim by putting a possessive arm around her naked shoulder and she wanted to shrug it off. But not in front of Vito. Instead, she snuggled into Max's hand, seeking some comfort as the disturbing past flooded back into her head.

'No. He ran away when he was a teenager and went back to the village where he was born,' she said in a quiet voice. She never talked about Vito or her past because there was so much in it she wanted to forget. It hurt. Only the present gave her a feeling of security. 'Vito was a difficult child,' she added resentfully. He had no right to disrupt her smoothly running life by turning up again.

'Anyone whose feelings lie deeper than surface level must be difficult for a butterfly brain to understand,' murmured Vito.

It was one of his taunting, Sicilian insults, and was meant to test the speed of her tongue rather than to be taken seriously. She knew that, from the tone. Max didn't. She'd opened her mouth with a ready answer, but Max stopped her, his voice ominous.

'No, Jolanda. Leave this to me.'

He made a great show of folding his arms aggressively and squaring up to the tall Sicilian. There was a sea of faces around them now and people were straining eagerly to hear.

Suddenly Jolanda saw how ludicrous they must seem. Max looked pompous and the guests gave the appearance of hyenas scenting a kill. There was a slight smile trying to break through Vito's carefully solemn mouth and a definite twinkle in his eye. He was secretly amused and she didn't blame him. This duel was between him and her; a family matter. It wasn't open to all comers.

Vito lifted a dark, sardonic brow to Jolanda.

'How submissive you are. You let your lover *speak* for you, as well as let him——'

'Stop there! You insolent scoundrel! I can't let you get away with rudeness to Joly,' cried Max indignantly.

'*Joly?*'

Vito's eyebrow crooked up even higher in derision and Jolanda inwardly squirmed. She did, in fact, hate Max's shortening of her name, but she'd never let Vito know that.

'It's a term of endearment,' she said sweetly.

Vito groaned and threw his head back in a gesture of theatrical despair. Jolanda thought he must know how tempting and tanned his throat was. He was displaying, for the women, like an exotic peacock.

'Have you English no finer senses? To call a beautiful woman "Joly",' he said, pained, 'is even worse than making love in a string vest.'

Her mouth twitched. Long ago, she'd secretly found it fun, sparring mentally with Vito, and she had forgotten how lively their rows had been. He was the only one who had a sharp enough wit to counter hers. She was itching to get back at him.

'I wouldn't know, I've never tried,' said Max tightly.

'Sorry. You looked the sort who might,' said Vito easily.

'He doesn't,' she said, with a sultry flutter of her lashes. 'Not when I'm around, anyway.'

Max blinked in astonishment, but basked in the murmurs around him. Jolanda smiled. Vito's brief, involuntary scowl made her feel she'd won a victory. He'd always been tight-lipped about her boyfriends, as if she belonged to him, in the same way that a Sicilian brother felt it his duty to protect the honour of his sister. He hated it when she referred obliquely to the possibility that she might have lovers.

'Still for sale?' murmured Vito.

'Still hiring?' she countered.

His eyes mocked. 'I never pay my way.'

'Neither do I. That makes us——'

'Twins?' he finished.

Jolanda whitened.

'Sorry,' he said smoothly and insincerely. 'Have I reminded you of someone you'd forgotten?'

'You bastard!' she breathed.

He knew damn well that he'd reminded her of the hollow in her life which wouldn't go away, that sense of never quite feeling whole again. And of his part in creating it. It had been a double bereavement: losing Nick and... She closed her mind to the memories. But she made a mistake in looking back at him. Her distraught eyes met his and saw sympathy there. That threw her and she floundered for a moment.

'Look here, Velardi——' began Max belligerently.

'Stay out of this,' hissed Jolanda, her eyes flashing dangerously. 'Vito, if you're here to ask me to make it up with Nick, then forget it. He's doing everything he can to hurt my father and to vilify him. I won't be disloyal.'

'What on earth makes you think I'd want to bring you two together?' he asked. 'You'd both begin to do something useful with that construction company. It might become competition for Velardi Construction. Surely it's better for me that all expansion is frozen because the two major shareholders can never agree?'

He was right. And she was offended at his reading of the situation, as far as the construction company was concerned. She and Nick met twice a year in her boardroom in the City and spent all day arguing. His plans were never financially secure and usually dominated by his passion for construction in Sicily. That was fraught with difficulties. She was the one with the cool business head. It irritated her that they had to compromise by working on small schemes in England that he didn't object to.

It was just as well it wasn't her main source of income. If she didn't freelance as a property agent for her father, she'd find her bills hard to meet.

Vito was giving her a quizzical look, as if he wanted her to pursue the subject. Jolanda was curious. He never drew breath without a hidden purpose, never flicked an eyelid, or arranged that darn cigar in his top pocket without a conscious striving for effect.

'Why are you here, then?' she asked flatly.

'You disappoint me, Jolanda,' he murmured. 'Isn't it more amusing to guess? To follow the clues, and work it out for yourself? I remember you once liked to play games. Are they all now solely for the bedroom?'

'Where else?' she parried, thinking how astounded he would be to learn that she was ridiculously ignorant about the realities of sex. If he ever found out, she thought ruefully, he'd have a vicious weapon to taunt her with and would make sure all her friends knew she had no experience of men beyond first base. That would ruin the image she'd carefully built up, of a hard-headed woman of the world. It even protected her from men. They thought she rejected them because they didn't meet her high standards.

When a man dated her, and was spurned, he usually tried to save face by hinting to his friends of the passionate night they'd shared. And so each one perpetuated the myth that Jolanda Docherty had given herself enthusiastically. But the vulnerable Jolanda had a terrible fear of committing herself to a man and then being abandoned. It wasn't too difficult to work out why. All the men in her early life had let her down in one way or another.

'All right, give me a clue,' she demanded.

Vito reached into his pocket and withdrew the black silk handkerchief he always carried, then boldly pushed it into Jolanda's cleavage. He took his time.

'Clue Number One,' he said in a gravelly voice.

She'd done nothing to stop him. On the contrary, she'd wanted the contact with his gently probing fingers to continue. There was something about his touch which had lit a few fires inside her.

He, rot him, was the same: cynical and unaffected as ever.

'You've come to help me make a clean breast of it?' she asked brightly.

Vito roared with laughter, his white teeth dazzling them all in his tanned face. Jolanda saw some of the women preen themselves. They'd be sorry, if they tangled with him.

'Close,' grinned Vito.

'Too close. Move away, your aftershave is overpowering,' she retorted.

A red-faced Max turned angrily to Jolanda. 'Do you want this…adopted brother of yours to stay?' he asked, his mouth grim.

She raised a bored eyebrow. Indifference was her best defence. It always had been.

'He doesn't bother me,' she said absently. 'He might amuse our guests.'

Amuse! He'd probably corrupt them all before the evening was out. Vito moved in sinister company, according to her father. Vito had seen it all, heard it all, done it all. Rumour had it that he enjoyed teaching what he'd learnt to others. Jolanda saw Charlotte slick her tongue over her lips and tried not to acknowledge the twinge of jealousy and anger within her.

'I'll do my best,' promised Vito with an unnerving menace.

Somehow she couldn't cope any longer with all that charisma and suppressed vitality which seeped so seductively from every one of Vito's golden pores.

'Come on, Max, let's dance,' she said.

Relieved to be out of sight, yet feeling as if the sun had gone behind a cloud when she left Vito, she dragged Max off through the crowd. They arrived at a cleared space on deck where a small band played, and began to rumba expertly. But in her head, with impeccable rhythm, beat an insistent refrain: *Vito's back in London, Vito's back in London.*

While she danced, her eyes constantly darted to the places where he might appear, unhappily conscious of the fact that he'd lifted the excitement in the air a few notches. Max, the band, the boat and the dancing didn't please her any more. The prospect of fencing with Vito had.

Suddenly his dark head and gorgeous bronzed face showed up above the bobbing heads. Jolanda sighed. She hated him, but found him hard to resist. For her, the sun had come out from the cloud. She knew how damaging it could be, standing in the relentless glare of the sun, but she couldn't prevent herself from wanting to bask in its life-giving rays.

Her deep brown eyes noted that Vito seemed to have a collection of women in tow. They were chattering animatedly, each one trying to get his attention. He was looking down on them with an expression of mild sexual interest on his face. A frown darkened Jolanda's face. He'd always been an effortlessly fast worker without even raising a little finger.

Jolanda quickly swept her eyes back to Max, placing one hand on his shoulder and executing a very sexy manoeuvre. From under her lashes she saw that her gyrations had done nothing for Vito, but plenty for Max. He pulled her roughly against his body and kissed her very thoroughly, his hands rotating around her swinging hips.

As usual, staying stone-cold sober with kisses, she didn't shut her eyes. Over Max's shoulder, she saw Vito quietly noting her lack of concentration, a faintly amused look on his face, a whisky in one hand and Charlotte's shoulder beneath the other. Most of the rest of Charlotte was pressed firmly into Vito's body. He must be aware, by now, that the woman didn't wear any underwear.

She'd never hated him more.

Charlotte wriggled, so that Vito's fingers now touched the upper swell of her heaving breast. He didn't respond, apart from letting his eyes crinkle a little more when they looked directly at Jolanda, as if they both shared some kind of secret.

Embarrassed, she shut her lids tightly and wished that she could enjoy kissing. Max seemed to. Many men had liked kissing her and that seemed odd because she couldn't be much fun for them. To her it was nothing more interesting than someone's mouth moving over yours and pressing harder and harder.

She'd tried to like it, with all the desperation of any woman who was tortured by her own lack of response. Even with Max, though, the man she might eventually marry, who was someone she really enjoyed being with, she felt no release of sensuality. She often wondered if all women were involved in a huge hoax by not telling each other that sex did nothing for them, either. Perhaps she and womankind were doomed to act for the rest of their lives.

Because Vito was there, she found herself twining her hands in Max's hair with a little more enthusiasm than usual, and hating herself for doing so. She was being false to herself, and unfair to Max. She dropped her hands and pushed against his shoulders to end the kiss.

'Darling!' Max surfaced, visibly shaken. 'I could kiss you all night. You make the world stand still for me.'

Jolanda winced inside, particularly as she knew Vito's sharp ears were picking up Max's fervent declaration. Out of the corner of her eye, she could see Charlotte trying to excite Vito by running her hands over his chest. He was ignoring her and thus driving her crazy. It always worked, she thought sourly.

'Joly? Are you listening?'

'Yes, Max,' she said quickly, focusing on his serious face. With a shock, she realised he had that look all men adopted when they were going to propose. Plenty had, thinking her reticence would disappear.

Max kissed her again, avidly, wrapping her in his arms so that she couldn't see Vito any more. When Max drew back, he kept her firmly clasped to his body and she tried not to mind as she stared straight at his out-of-focus nose and wondered if she was going cross-eyed.

'I know your father is wealthy, Jolanda,' began Max. 'But I'm quite a whizz-kid in the City.' His face had flushed with pride. 'If I keep my nose to the grindstone for the next few years——' He broke off, at Jolanda's swallowed laugh. Max was sounding formal and odd; almost verging on the ridiculous. 'Something wrong?' he frowned.

'Neck-ache,' she said truthfully, glad when he gave her a little more living space. It was a hot evening and Max was sweating quite heavily by now. Odd how all men seemed rather graceless beside Vito.

'Anyway,' he continued. 'I reckon I could make use of my contacts and become as sharp an operator as your father is. I admire him. He doesn't allow sentiment to get in his way. That's how to do business. Same as you. You've got a reputation for having a nose for a shrewd deal.'

More noses. Jolanda tried to keep her mind on what he was saying.

'Are you trying to tell me something?' she asked absently, wondering how important it was to Max that she was Stan Docherty's daughter. Max was a property speculator too. A tiny trickle of resentment flitted through her head. No one seemed to want her for herself alone. There was always a catch to it.

'Oh, well, yes. I'm telling you that with a little help, my future's assured.'

'A little help. I suppose you could be useful to Father,' she said cautiously, testing him.

Max's face lit up. 'Darling! I know I could! Do you think he'd take me on? Joly, I know hundreds of men must have said this to you, but I—— Hell! What's going on?'

His dazed eyes were focusing on the bank. Jolanda felt a jolt as the steamer moved abruptly into reverse and then chugged steadily away from its mooring. She saw with astonishment that someone had released the ropes which secured the boat to the quayside.

Her eyes lit with glee and she turned unerringly to look up at the wheelhouse. Vito waved at her. The coloured lights strung around the deck began to swing. She was convulsed with laughter as couples began to stagger at the violent motion and glasses and plates on the deck began to slide into the river.

Without a word, she slipped off her spindly high heels and left the spluttering Max, who seemed incapable of seeing the joke. In her bare feet, she padded up the steep steps to the wheelhouse.

Vito unlocked the door, bowed, and let her in, then locked the door again. He reached for a lever in front of him and slammed it to one side. The boat shuddered and with a loud rush of protesting water and a tremendous roar of engines it ground forwards, the movement throwing Jolanda off balance and into Vito's conveniently waiting arms.

'What are you up to?' she asked suspiciously, trying to disentangle herself.

'Amusing your guests, as you requested.'

'By tipping them into the Thames?' she queried, seeing one or two lurching towards the rail.

He chuckled. 'Livened things up a bit, didn't it, my little *cassata*?'

A rush of memories momentarily stopped her from answering. As a child, he'd called her *cassata*. She'd adored ice-cream with candied fruit and he always let her eat his portion, feeding her from his own spoon. Her eyes met his and she knew he remembered too, with some tenderness. It was a bitter-sweet memory. Like being in his arms. Like seeing him smile.

He did that rarely. When he bestowed that exceptional, open smile on someone, his eyes twinkled and lost their hard, glittering look. His face relaxed, becoming soft and friendly instead of carved in cold bronze.

Her lips parted and his high-arched mouth lost its cynical curve and grew full and sensual. With the honour of *that* smile came danger and delight.

Jolanda didn't try to escape from his firm, confident grasp. That would look as if she found his proximity unnerving. She looked up at him and arched a carefully brushed eyebrow.

'Still mad, bad and dangerous to know,' she commented drily. 'Do you actually know how to steer this thing?'

He clapped a hand to his forehead.

'*Mamma mia!* I forgot!' he cried dramatically, pushing her aside.

'Nobody, but nobody, says *Mamma mia*,' reproved Jolanda, watching the scene with interest.

The boat was heading for a huge Thames barge. Everyone on the steamer was shouting and Max could be seen pounding up the stairs to the wheelhouse, his face black with fury.

'They do in bad movies,' said Vito in a conversational tone.

'Boy, is this becoming one!' grinned Jolanda.

Calmly, Vito corrected the steamer's course, nodded politely to Max who was now banging angrily on the door, and began to shrug off his jacket. Jolanda helped. The faintly fragrant warmth from Vito's male body filled her senses. She let her fingers rest briefly on his biceps as she wriggled the jacket off. Then she beamed through the glass at Max.

'Fabulous party!' she yelled. 'Clever surprise of yours!'

'Let me in!' shouted Max.

She pulled on the door and flung open her hands in defeat. Max's mouth compressed, but he apparently decided to make the best of the situation. His guests were laughing and gesturing up to Vito as if they were finding this the best part of the evening so far. Max wouldn't risk losing face.

'I'll try to find a crowbar or something,' Max yelled.

Jolanda did the decent thing and waited until he'd gone and then let out peals of laughter, leaning back weakly against the bulkhead.

'You ruined everything for him,' said Jolanda, feeling sorry for Max, who couldn't hope to compare favourably to the exotic, wicked and unconventional Vito.

'Oh, I thought he was doing a pretty good job of ruining his own chances without my help,' he answered drily. 'I do dislike clumsiness, don't you?'

Her eyes slanted at him, and she inwardly agreed. Max should never have mixed ambition with emotion. It was offensive.

'What clumsiness?' she asked, wide-eyed.

'For a start, choosing a moment to ask you something when your attention was elsewhere,' he said with maddening truth. 'Would you have accepted?'

'Accepted what?' she asked, curiously pleased that he'd been so perceptive and knew what Max was planning to say.

'Well, I think your lover was going to ask you for your father's hand in marriage,' he said in a deadpan voice.

Bubbling laughter escaped from Jolanda before she could control it.

'Business is business,' she said firmly.

'A proposal of marriage is business?'

'Why not? It makes sense to be realistic and practical. Passion only lasts a short while. Business partnerships can endure longer.'

Vito's eyes narrowed. 'Real passion lasts forever. You haven't met it yet. Or if you have, you haven't recognised it,' he said quietly.

'You delude yourself, Vito. Your passion lasts for as long as it takes to get a woman's clothes off and make love to her. Hardly the stuff a lifetime of desire is made of,' she scorned.

'You shouldn't judge my emotions by yours,' he said quietly.

'You shouldn't listen in to other people's conversations,' she rebuked.

'How else am I to know everything that goes on?' he asked in astonishment. 'Don't accept a business proposal. Don't end up with Max. Think of all those boardroom executives and their bored wives, the duty dinners and conversations about share prices. It would be so dull! You'd be joining the Foreign Legion within a month of marriage, Jolanda. Or should I call you...Joly?'

She pummelled him, as she had when a child. But now she felt the change from the once wiry body to the muscle-packed strength of a full grown man and her fists dropped to her side.

'Maybe I'd like all that,' she said, diverting her senses.

'If his proposal bores you and makes your eyes glaze over, what do you think the next seventy years are going to be like?'

She made a face. 'Seventy years! It sounds like a prison sentence. I don't think I could live with anyone for that long. Could you?'

Vito gave a secretive smile. 'Depends on whether we survive this voyage or not.'

'Where are we going?' she joked, her eyes dancing. 'Never-never land?'

'Is that where you'd like to go, Jolanda?' asked Vito softly. 'To a fairy-tale land where children never grow up?'

She sobered when his solemn eyes flickered to hers and she felt herself in danger of falling hopelessly beneath his spell. She wouldn't let him hurt her again. She was completely in control of her own life, assertive, confident. She was tough and cold-hearted. This was a party and she was going to have Fun. It was up to her to keep this brief meeting light and frothy, with the occasional scything verbal defence.

'Too late,' she cried, flinging her hand dramatically across her forehead. 'I'm a child no more. Lines have already appeared. I'm cracking up. The ageing process has begun.'

To her consternation, Vito leaned back towards her, lightly touching her naked, vulnerable shoulder in a knee-trembling caress. Jolanda felt a tantalising *frisson* as his fingers travelled over her satin-smooth skin and knew he was taking pleasure in the sensation. He was a first-class sensualist.

'Can't see it,' he said, his mouth so close that Jolanda strained imperceptibly to catch the fragrance of his breath. 'Your face is perfectly flawless. Though, I confess, I do detect a change in your body.'

In looking down, he'd dropped his long lashes on to his cheekbones and Jolanda felt a pain slicing into her stomach. God! How she remembered watching him sleeping; creeping into his room early in the mornings and holding her breath in suspense and awe!

'Darn it! You've noticed my wooden leg?' she said.

She pretended to sulk, her nerves strung taut. She was used to men admiring her body but had never been as highly aware of her own sexuality as she was now, with Vito's frank and open stare directed down her body-hugging strapless dress.

Or rather what was inside, and overflowing it. Jolanda felt her breasts lift, rising and falling rapidly with her increased rate of breathing. There seemed to be an electric storm crackling across the small gap between them, and she was getting the worst of it. Every inch of her flesh had been charged with a tingling current.

'Jolanda! How disappointing. You've become slow in your repartee. It must be the company you keep. If we're on the Peter Pan and Wendy theme, shouldn't that be a hooked hand?' he murmured. 'And in any case, you could have two wooden legs for all I know. Those cushion-soft curves prevent me from seeing any further than your cleavage.'

With a quick movement, he abandoned her abruptly and turned his attention back to steering the steamer.

Jolanda swallowed and wondered why he hadn't taken advantage of the situation and kissed her. Any other red-blooded man would.

'I'm the same size I was at sixteen,' she defended.

She could have kicked herself as soon as the words
were out, inwardly groaning at the provocative way she'd
said them. Her voice was husky and inviting. Why did
she have to be like a thousand other women and run
after Vito Velardi? She knew what contempt he felt for
them all.

'Mmm. The parcel might be the same size, but you
know what to do with the contents now,' he said mildly.

'Well it's not addressed to you, so leave it alone.'

Jolanda didn't know whether she felt pleased or offended. It was a sexist remark, wasn't it? She certainly
felt disconcerted that he had noted her attractions and
yet found the steamer more interesting. His sharp eyes
were scanning the river as if she didn't exist, and she
was in her sexiest dress!

'I intend to. It's not my practice to pick up a package
not destined for me. Besides, any parcel wrapped as
gaudily and as intriguingly as yours gets handled by a
number of men,' murmured Vito, staring ahead intently.
'That increases the risk of it coming undone and looking
shabby after it's been knocking around for a while. What
a shame that damaged goods are worthless to the final
recipient.'

'You insolent bastard!' she gasped.

'You do disappoint me, reverting to plain abuse. I can
see I'm going to have to take up your education, as far
as insults are concerned. You've lost all your finesse.'

'I call a spade a spade in my daily life,' she snapped.

'How incredibly boring. Never mind, you'll soon get
the hang of reviling me properly,' he said in a kindly,
fatherly tone.

'I wish you'd tell me why you're here,' she said crossly.

It annoyed her that he was still able to treat her like
a kid sister, despite the fact that she was a successful

businesswoman in her own right. She'd never lose that image in his eyes, no matter what she looked like.

In her annoyance, Jolanda recognised her old enemy: jealousy. She and Vito had quarrelled about her possessiveness once. Now she didn't care about anyone much, but the jealousy was still there. Like a sulky child, she wanted Vito to adore her so that she could spurn him. She was behaving in an immature way.

It was time she realised that it was better not to be the object of his attentions. He'd reduced all her friends to weeping wrecks, after all, with his cruelty.

'I'm here for the same reason as you,' he drawled. 'To have fun.'

'You never had proper fun in your life,' she snapped.

'True. Only the improper kind. It's the best sort to indulge in. But you don't have to walk around with a grin on your face to have fun,' he answered. 'I get my kicks secretly. They're more enjoyable that way. All you need is a capacity to live life to the full. As we're going to do,' he said, a sudden mischievous grin blinding her in the semi-darkness of the wheelhouse.

Spurts of excitement leapt within her. She knew that wicked look in his eyes well. It had prefaced many an adventure.

'You can't just sweep in here and take me over. Max is giving this party for me,' she began.

'And I'm giving this party for us,' he answered, holding her eyes with his. 'Do you want to fly, Wendy, and go on the Great Adventure, or stay in the dog kennel with Nanna?'

Jolanda's treacherous lips refused to stay pressed together. They quirked, and then split into a huge grin.

'You're being unfair to Max,' she managed.

'Of course,' he answered smoothly. 'I never play fair. There's a famous Italian handbook on playing cards. It begins with the first rule: always try to see your opponents' cards. Well? Shall we fly away from boredom? Let some magic into our lives?'

'We need fairy-dust. I see no Tinkerbell,' she chuckled.

'It's her night off,' said Vito blandly. 'Here we are. Watch this for a bit of neat docking.'

Alarmed at the rate at which they were approaching a brightly lit jetty festooned with balloons and flags, Jolanda clutched at his sleeve and was immediately hauled into his side so that they stood hip to hip. She trembled.

'Don't worry,' he reassured her. 'I've never done this before.'

'Oh, that's all right then,' she said faintly.

The engine growled into reverse. Vito snatched up his jacket and unlocked the door, thrusting Jolanda down the stairs, passing Max on the way.

'You'd better take over,' Vito flung over his shoulder as he raced for the side of the steamer, hauling Jolanda with him. 'There's an irate-looking man in a peaked cap coming up the Thames.'

'Vito—Max——'

Jolanda struggled half-heartedly. She wanted to go with Vito, but the look on Max's face upset her.

'*Jump!*'

'Oh, my God!'

Jolanda found herself in an iron grip, then in mid-air, and the hard wooden deck of the jetty came up to meet her. She rolled with Vito in a tangle of threshing arms and legs, intensely aware of the hardness of his body and the contrasting softness of hers.

His hands seemed to be everywhere. For a moment, they lay still, breathless, their bodies entwined, and she knew he was going to kiss her. And hoped so.

CHAPTER TWO

DISAPPOINTMENT and relief filled her mind when, for some inexplicable reason, he didn't kiss her. Jolanda began to doubt her intuition as far as Vito was concerned. She'd been so sure. Instead, he was giving her one of his mocking smiles and she wondered if he was teasing her. She sat up to see Max wrestling with the controls of the steamer as it ploughed backwards, towards an unnervingly official-looking launch.

'Admire the decorations quickly,' urged Vito, 'then we must dash. I'm afraid Tinkerbell didn't leave me enough fairy-dust. Our flying wasn't up to much, was it? Quick!'

Jolanda opened her mouth, protesting loudly as he hauled her on to her feet and began to drag her towards a cigar-shaped open-top sports-car.

'Like the balloons?' persisted Vito.

She blinked. Impatient, he picked her up and slid her expertly into the car. There were long streamers and flags all around the jetty and the balloons bore the words 'Clue Number Two'.

'Love them. What——'

Vito reached across, his eyes smiling into hers and she shrank back into the seat at the full blast of his sexuality which hit her insides like a mix of fizzy champagne and potent scrumpy.

His arm came around her body and he slowly clipped in her seatbelt. She felt like a wild animal, trapped and frightened, watching the hunter approach.

Vito's eyes glowed, hypnotising her. His hot breath made her upper lip tingle and she wanted to rub it, preferably against his, but pride prevented her. He'd know that her skin had been sensitised and go for the kill. He must have done this countless times. Once, long ago, he must have calculated how long he could take to fasten a seatbelt and get the maximum sensuality out of it. A thousand women must have sat like this, she thought resentfully, wondering how many took advantage of his nearness and wrapped their arms around his neck.

He moved away and she was furious with herself for being sorry.

'Vito,' she said angrily. 'You must let me—ohhh!'

She was thrust back into the seat by the force of the car's acceleration. A band new E-type Jag. Heaven. The wind sent her hair blowing back like a black, turbulent river and she discovered that her face was wreathed in smiles.

'Max will never forgive you,' she called into the wind.

Vito joined the evening traffic, appearing to drive by instinct, like a true Italian, enjoying the challenge as if he were hurtling around a Roman arena in a film version of *Ben Hur*.

'More to the point, will he forgive you?' he asked mockingly.

'There's nothing to forgive,' she said haughtily. 'Anyone could see I was forced to go with you.'

He skilfully threaded the car through several lanes of traffic and stopped sharp on a double yellow line, oblivious to the irate drivers around him.

'You can't park here!' she cried in irritation. He needn't bring his foreign disregard of rules into her life.

'It's perfectly safe. You reckon that you were forced to come?'

'You know I was!'

'Out you get, then. Be quick, before the car's impounded. It doesn't belong to me. Leap out and find your way back to Max. I imagine he's been stopped in mid-channel by the river police and is busy explaining how the boat was hijacked. Off you go.'

With a primming of her mouth, and a great deal of inner reluctance, Jolanda opened the car door and stepped out, realising suddenly she was barefoot. It didn't matter. How she'd get back on to the boat, she didn't know. She turned to walk away.

'Don't you want to know about Clue Number Three?'

She paused, puzzled. What *had* he meant by teasing her with clues, as if they were on a treasure hunt? A thought hit her. He must have stage-managed the whole business, setting up the flags and so on, the balloons, getting them printed...

'Get in,' he urged. 'Or it'll melt.'

Astounded and fascinated, her sense of fun overcoming her scruples, she scrambled back into the car.

'Melt?'

She took the precaution of doing up her own seatbelt this time as Vito nodded vigorously and swept the car boldly back into the flow of traffic.

Jolanda settled comfortably into the seat. Reckless though he seemed, she always had felt safer with Vito driving than any other man she'd known. And, of course, in far more danger with him.

'What melts, Jolanda, apart from you in the arms of your lovers?'

She ignored his taunt because she'd had an inspiration.

'Chocolate fireguards.'

'Keep on the food theme.'

'Ice-cream,' she said smugly. '*Cassata* ice-cream.'

'Correct.' He glanced at his watch. 'Almost there.'

'Another party?' she hazarded.

'Nothing so banal.'

'Oh, good.'

Despite herself, Jolanda was fatalistically intrigued. They parked—legally—by a high wall. Vito leapt out of the car and unlocked a small door in the wall. He came back to the car and picked her up.

That was twice in one evening, she thought, as he strode towards the door. She'd never been picked up by a man before and adored it, feeling both sexy and female at the same time.

One of her hands rested lightly on Vito's hard chest; the other had curved up to lie within inches of his dark gold throat. The temptation to touch his skin was overwhelming. But she refused to give in to his blatant manoeuvring. If only she knew what he was up to!

'Would you be carrying me if I were a little old lady?' she asked tartly, defusing the situation.

'If you were a little old lady, you wouldn't have taken your shoes off and hurried to be my accomplice,' he said logically. 'So there'd be no need to save your bare feet from London's filthy pavements.'

'If that's the only reason you're carrying me, then,' she retorted coolly, 'you can stop that hand from caressing my bottom.'

Vito's eyes widened as if in surprise.

'So it is! Sorry. Habit,' he explained blandly.

He slid her down to a stone path. They were in a silent, Italianate garden, mysterious in the dark and overburdened with ghostly-looking statues and niches containing laurel-crowned emperors in white marble.

'Find the ice-cream,' he ordered.

'You have a definite sense of the ridiculous,' she said, laughing.

'And so do you,' he murmured.

That sounded too intimate, and linked them, so Jolanda sniffed in a disparaging way and set off.

The flowers in the garden were night-scented and releasing their perfumes as she brushed past, drowning her senses and slowing her up. She ambled along the paths which were overhung with fragrant blossom, her bare feet bruising the herbs which grew in cracks between the stones. Vito stayed close behind, his breathing warm and even on her neck.

The image of his body behind her was imprinted on her mind, tantalising her. Her own breathing had become deep and jerky. Vito was creating a magical situation, spiriting her away from the cold rat-race she'd lived in for the last few years. It was unsettling. But disturbingly irresistible.

In the centre of the garden was a pond and in the centre of the pond on a tiny island rose an exuberantly carved stone fountain. Balanced precariously on it was a huge silver salver.

Jolanda's delighted face turned to Vito's.

'I've found it,' she said softly. It was silly, it was bizarre, and she loved it, whatever he was setting up for her.

For a moment he was silent, his face in the shadow apart from his left cheekbone and jaw, both of which looked oddly tense.

'I'm afraid I have, too,' he growled in a husky voice.

'You mean this is the end of the clues?' she said, not hiding her disappointment.

'No.' He stepped into the light and she saw that he was his usual cynical self. 'This, I think, is the beginning. Go and get it.'

'How deep is the pond?'

'Find out.'

He leaned back against a statue of Apollo and folded his arms. Apollo came to life. Tinted golden, given a dash of style and a hint of wicked sensuality. Jolanda swallowed.

She hesitantly put one foot in the water. It was pleasantly warm and silky from the warmth of the day and she slid the foot further. Her toes didn't touch the bottom until the water had reached above her knees. She pushed her skirt up to her thighs and stepped right in, wading boldly across to the little island. The silver dish was out of her reach.

'Climb up, Jolanda.'

She paused, aware of the spectacle he was being treated to, as the silvery water ran off her slender legs. There was something terribly sexy about it all. If she were to climb that darn fountain, he'd get even more of an eyeful. But Vito's appearance in her life had revitalised her and she felt quite abandoned.

If she hammed it up, she could get away with giving in to her wantonness. With a mock sultry glance over her naked shoulder, she slowly wriggled her skirt higher and placed one foot on the first stone cupid's head. Vito let out a low whistle. Pleased, she reached up for a handhold.

'A true social climber,' he called.

Jolanda threw him a scathing look. 'Story of my life,' she said calmly. 'I climb to the top and lesser men look on.'

'The top always looks better from below. You don't see the accumulated grime,' he retorted. 'It's disappointing when you get there. Besides, I've been up there before you.'

'But didn't have the staying power,' she commented.

He began to softly hum the tune of 'The Stripper'. Jolanda moved easily up the fountain in time to the erotic, jerky rhythm, collecting the dish and posing on top with a few outlandish thrusts of her hips as Vito's laughing voice began to sing the last refrain.

She saw with delight that someone had scrawled with a food dye in copperplate writing across the *cassata*, 'Clue Number Three. Oh, and Four'.

Like a waiter at the Ritz—apart from her giggling—she bore the tray back across the pool. Vito helped her out and led her to an arbour. Someone had laid up a circular table there, with a lace cloth, sparkling silver and cut glass.

'Strawberries and champagne. How incredibly unoriginal, Vito,' she mocked, placing the ice-cream on the elegantly laid table as he opened the champagne. Candles made the silver cutlery glow and the glasses glittered with the flickering flames.

'You think they're unoriginal? That rather depends, my little mountain goat, on what you do with the strawberries and what I do with the champagne,' he murmured wickedly.

Jolanda lifted an eyebrow. Vito's sexual experience was vast and varied. He must have indulged in all kinds of amusements. Her mind raced with possibilities and, innocent that she was, she blushed, trying to work out what he meant. She'd walked into that one.

'Stand still.'

He knelt on one knee like a troubador before his lady
and began to dry her legs. Jolanda bit her lip in the
partial darkness, one hand resting on his shoulder for
support as he carefully wiped between each toe, and
gazing helplessly down on his broad back. And then
came the slow, gentle rasp of the soft towel on her calves,
the backs of her knees, and finally her thighs. Was it
her imagination, or was he taking an unusually long time
to dry her there?

Her jaw was clamped tight against the wonderful sensations chasing up her body and rushing back to her toes
again. With elaborate politeness and still on one knee,
Vito pulled down the hem of her dress again. Slowly.
She must be almost as reluctant as he was.

'We eat the ice-cream. Half for you, half for me,' he
said huskily, looking up at her.

She longed to reach down and caress his face. His eyes
looked huge and quite tender. Something in her past
tugged at her memory. Had he looked at her like that
before? For a confusing, muddled moment, she thought
that his hands were on her hips, stroking, then he had
risen and walked away to his seat beneath the scented
roses.

'You used to give me all your share,' she said with a
false heartiness, slipping jauntily into the seat beside him.

'I give nothing away now.'

She shot him a puzzled glance. Was he deliberately
teasing her by being enigmatic, or was he genuinely secretive? She sighed.

'You Sicilians! You're as open as a bank vault.'

With a vigorous slash of the pastry knife, she divided
the ice-cream. The knife hit something bumpy at the
bottom.

'Oh, Vito!' she whispered. It was a silver charm. Twins.

Her heart lurched hopelessly as she thought of Nick. Quarrelling with him had left such emptiness within her. It was as if part of her no longer existed. Having a twin brother meant you and he weren't two people, but one, divided.

Through their childhood, Nick had drifted away from her, dazzled by the outlandish behaviour of the rebellious Vito. For some reason, Vito had always borne a grudge against her father.

There had been quarrels from the start. Only her mother was able to intercede and halt the cold, lashing cynicism of the young Vito and soothe the quick-tempered Stan Docherty. Jolanda and Nick had watched wide-eyed when the battles raged, horrified that Vito should question anything their father did, or that the sullen boy should refuse to make any attempt to please him.

Yet all through the rows Vito was guarded, as if curbing an inner rage and choosing his words carefully. He wounded her father, she could see that, even if half of Vito's insults went over her head. In turn her father reviled Vito, taking a pleasure in finding ways to criticise him in front of guests.

She had seen Vito with an implacable smile, never showing by the flicker of an eyelid that the ridicule upset him. And with that same implacable smile he always managed to let out an innocent remark which embarrassed her father or showed him up in some way and brought a gasp of shock from them all.

She'd resented the fact that Vito wilfully disturbed the family serenity, and tried to tell herself that the beatings he had from her father were deserved. She had to side with her father. He adored her, gave her presents, fussed over her.

But Vito had his revenge. It was to poison Nick's mind against his own father.

After many attempts to run away and join Vito, Nick finally made it at the age of eighteen. But not before he told his father exactly what he thought of him and his business ethics. Jolanda had been shocked and dismayed that her brother should be so biting and cruel, so ungrateful. The business had given them a comfortable life, after all. Nick's terrible accusations against their father, fed by Vito's lies, and Nick's desertion of *her*, had ripped apart the bonds which bound the twins.

But the bonds were still there, and she was their prisoner. Being a twin was a different relationship from any other. She needed Nick, to be whole. Yet it was up to him to make his peace with her and her father, since he'd caused the rift. Not Vito. It was annoying that Vito always took it on himself to solve people's problems— usually for his own reasons. She fixed him with cold eyes and handed him the tiny silver figures, posing so lovingly together.

'A rather heavy-handed hint. I really must give you lessons in subtlety,' she said sarcastically. 'I thought you said you weren't trying to plead Nick's cause... Oh, Vito!' she exclaimed, her voice becoming scolding. 'You're infuriating!'

He wasn't listening to a word she was saying. He was twining flowers in her hair, a look of concentration on his face.

'Clue Number Five,' he said softly, picking up a scarlet poppy.

Jolanda's brow creased into a frown, as she tried to solve the puzzle which persisted in nagging at her. He had moved close, his hands busy in her hair, fixing there wild poppies, marigolds, and daisies. Now in his hand appeared a stem of clover, the huge red flowers telling her that it couldn't have grown in England. She kept her breathing as regular as possible, with his mouth only inches from hers.

'I get the picture,' she said coldly. 'You're trying to make me think that I'll love it with Nick in Sicily, that it's full of ice-cream sellers, wild flowers and . . . well, I don't know what the balloons were all about. You're wasting your time.'

'Wrong. Think again. Look back in your memories,' he said, his voice low.

To her surprise, she began to be swamped by them, vague, terror-ridden ones, and that showed in her face. Jolanda had no wish to be vulnerable with a ruthless man like Vito around. Instead, she focused on his wretched clues, rather keen to prove she could follow his convoluted mind and was as clever as he was.

'A party, perhaps? The only thing I remember . . .'

Again her voice trailed away. This time, however, she wasn't irritated, but genuinely choking on her own emotions.

'Damn you, Vito Velardi!' she whispered. 'Damn you for resurrecting everything I want to forget!'

It had been her memory of her and Nick, stupidly clutching balloons, watching him through blurred vision leave home on their eleventh birthday. What timing Vito had! Dramatically extracting the last ounce of poignancy and pathos! It should have been a day of joy. But birthdays after that had become shadowy days of unhappy memories.

She knew then what he meant to her: that she'd been upset when Vito and her father argued because she loved them both; that all her fighting to keep her father supreme in her heart was because she feared that she loved Vito more, and that was surely wrong.

Even now, it hurt to recall the tears, the pleading; especially those from Nick. For good or bad, Vito had been the centre of their lives, his seven years' seniority and foreign glamour lending an exotic glitter to his lawlessness.

It had been a terrible time at home when he'd gone. Even her sweet mother had been irritable and there had been an air of reproach between her and her husband. When Vito left, Jolanda had thought she'd never see him again, and the wrench in her young life had been deeply wounding. Even more wounding had been the realisation that he was so important to her.

But there had been something else which had made his loss hard to bear. Whenever anyone went away, she'd noticed that she felt an unnamed dread which she'd never been able to pin-point; one which was irrational but rendered her hysterical inside. It always made her want to cry.

Even now, she was succumbing to it. A huge lump filling her throat and hot prickly tears threatening her composure, she turned away and buried her face in the honeysuckle which twined lovingly around the roses, trying to hold back her distress. But she found her unresisting body being drawn into Vito's chest and she lay her head there as she had when she was a child. And a yearning teenager.

His hand stroked her hair lightly.

'So there is a faint spark of humanity inside you,' he drawled.

Feeling betrayed by his heartless words, Jolanda flung herself away from him, but her wrist was gripped hard and her glance shot up to see how menacing and glittering his eyes were.

'Face it,' he growled. 'Remember. Remember how it was. The fear. The screams, the dust, the pressure on your lungs, the pain in your head.'

'What are you talking about?' she asked in astonishment. There was nothing of that in her past, and yet he seemed unusually serious.

He shook her roughly. 'You have to do it, Jolanda!'

For a brief moment she recalled the sensation of being unable to breathe, and her frightened gaze was held by his piercing, blazing eyes.

'You remember something,' he muttered. 'Think, Jolanda!'

'No...' she moaned, her head tipping back to avoid being mesmerised.

Then she shuddered in shock. She felt the softness of Vito's mouth on her vulnerable throat, moving savagely, preventing her from speaking, her own ecstatic inner responses effectively paralysing her.

His kisses ran along her jaw and his hand came up to clamp around her skull, forcing her head down. From beneath rapidly closing eyes she saw the infinite sensuality of his face and she gritted her teeth.

But his strong finger and thumb thrust down on her chin to open her mouth and suddenly it was filled with sensation which almost made her want to sink into his arms instead of sitting stiff and defiant.

Expertly he kissed her, the intimacy of his tongue both sweet and seductively suggestive. She found herself trembling, shuddering against his skilful assault.

Far in the background of her consciousness, she heard the liquid notes of a nightingale and groaned. Nature had a way of conniving with Vito whenever he wanted something.

Jolanda's eyes jerked open and, with a quick shove, she pushed herself away from his marauding mouth.

'What are you after?' she asked harshly, her face as cold as stone. 'A swift knee in the groin?'

He flinched at her crudeness, as she'd meant him to. Beneath all of his biting sarcasm, he held idealistic images of women. No wonder he hadn't married, she thought morosely, considering the company he kept. He'd never find his perfect wife in the eager, insatiable female hordes who pursued him.

'I thought I was making it perfectly clear what I was after,' he said huskily, quickly recovering, one hand moving boldly up her thigh.

She slapped it hard and prised away his fingers one by one with a disdainful expression.

'Oh. Now I understand. It was another of your clues,' she said casually.

'You might say that.'

Vito stretched lazily as if her refusal to go along with his lovemaking didn't matter. Jolanda's mouth thinned.

'I also have a clue,' she said, with deceptive calm.

Vito looked interested.

Jolanda grabbed the bottle of champagne and poured it over his head. Instead of avoiding it, or catching hold of her arm to stop her, he sat beneath the glittering golden stream, eyeing her with consummate satisfaction.

He was saving face, she thought. He wouldn't deign to admit that she'd caught him off guard.

'If that isn't enough of a clue for you to guess how I feel about you, then I have a few ideas about using the strawberries, too,' she snapped.

With a grin at her threat, Vito slicked his tongue around her lips, sensually, delightedly tasting the champagne which poured down his face and which made his high cheekbones shine gold in the candle-light. The deep rivulets ran in sparkling streams on either side of his mouth. His dark hair had plastered into flat curls on his forehead.

Jolanda had a vivid image of him, emerging from the sea ten years ago like a Greek god: twenty-three, muscular, tanned. He'd returned on his first fleeting, disruptive visit from Sicily since leaving five years before. She and her girlfriends had never seen anything so beautiful in all their sixteen years, and it had been her first and only experience of really coveting a man and knowing he was unobtainable.

Weak with worship, she had remained seated on her beach towel. He was too handsome, too sure of himself. She'd decided to play it cool.

Her friends had rushed up to him, wide-eyed, fawning. And she knew from the way he gave them one of his remote, bored looks that they were like irritating insects to him. She'd lain back and let the sun heat her body, then had felt her skin tingling and known Vito must be near. The anticipation had made her burn inside, in places where she'd never imagined could ever feel any sensation.

At a splash of water on her cheek, she'd opened her eyes to see his dark face bending over her and he'd asked softly whether she'd like an ice-cream.

Jolanda smiled sadly. To him, she'd been just a kid, to be fed candy. She remembered the misery she'd felt and her response. 'No. I'd rather have you.' It had shocked him into silence. His teasing had stopped.

Now, he seemed to be deliberately teasing her again. She gave him a jaundiced look, privately longing to taste the champagne lingering on his skin. But she must keep her head. He certainly had an ulterior motive if he was paying her so much attention now. It must be quite important. Was it, in fact, anything to do with the construction company? Did he know something she didn't about trends in the market?

Perhaps it would pay her to play along with him. Her face showed her uncertainty. It might hurt her, when he revealed what his true motives were. Yet she needed to know!

'You always did have an insatiable curiosity, Jolanda,' he murmured, reading her mind successfully. 'Still enthralled? Ready for the next clue?'

'It's all getting rather tedious,' she said tartly. 'Can't you simply state your purpose and get it over with?'

'If you insist,' he said, moving close to her again and fixing her with desire-laden eyes. 'I want to make love to you.'

Jolanda suppressed the yearning voice which kept saying, 'Why not?' His triumph would be complete if he took her. Especially when he knew he'd taken an ageing virgin.

'No, you don't.'

'I could prove to you that I do,' he murmured. 'Give me your hand.'

'Vito, dear,' she said sweetly. 'It's precisely because you *say* that's what you want that I know it's merely a means to an end.'

'You misjudge me——'

'No, I don't. You're far too subtle to say outright what you really want. To you, part of the pleasure in life is to deceive others about your true purpose. Why not cut the cackle and be straight with me for a change?'

'Making love to you was to be my *pièce de résistance*,' he said, with a hurt expression and a little careful mockery of himself.

'I'd resist it,' she said drily.

Vito sighed. 'You see through me every time, don't you?' he said sadly.

Jolanda's chest rose in fury to hear him admit that her suspicions were correct and that he'd had an ulterior motive in pretending to seduce her. It was a despicable thing to do, using sex for his own dark purposes. She loathed being manipulated by him.

'You're like a Grand Master of chess,' she snapped, 'pushing people around like pawns on a chessboard. You do it to all of us and it's insulting.' She stood up. 'Take me home. I don't want to see you again.'

'Why? We were having an amusing time, weren't we?' he enquired.

Jolanda bit her lip. How shallow he was.

'I have remembered, as you wanted me to. I remember how vicious and ruthless you are, how you set out to get your own way by deceit and flattery and false charm. I remember how you broke all the rules in the book to avenge yourself on people who'd slighted you in some way. And I don't want to be associated with you. Father has disowned you and so have I.'

Vito, outwardly courteous as ever, had risen with her and now stood contemplating her angry face and flashing eyes. There was a dangerous brooding stillness about his pose and Jolanda prepared to start throwing the china if he didn't let her leave.

She could never cope when he began to simmer. Deep beneath the surface was a volcanic temper. It had terrified them all, friends and enemies alike, her father, she and Nick, and a handful of headmasters unfortunate enough to cross the sullen, unsmiling, uncompromising Vito.

In his early youth he'd been as cold as a stone and utterly unresponsive to any overtures, his only gentleness being towards her bed-ridden mother.

Dark, olive-skinned and tough, he'd stood out everywhere he went. His sharp eyes and quick reflexes made him a star on the sports field; his refusal to let anyone into his life made him a remotely admired god.

That was until he discovered sex, thought Jolanda. He seemed to be using it even in those days, to get his own back on the human race. What was the chip on his shoulder? The mere fact that he'd been adopted.

'Why were you so ungrateful to my father?' she blurted out. 'He took you in, called you his son——'

'I had no wish to be the son of a cheat and a liar,' he said proudly.

'How dare you talk about my father like that?' cried Jolanda. 'He never complained when your teachers said they'd beaten you more times than anyone in their lives for insolence. He never said anything about your diabolical school reports——'

'Your ice-cream has melted,' he muttered harshly.

She glanced down. 'You never finish an argument decently!' she yelled. She picked up the plate and threw it at him. He ducked successfully, but was coming for her and she thought better of standing up to him in his present mood. She ran.

Vito ran faster. He swung her around, the weight of his body carrying her downwards on to the soft mattress of a sun-lounger.

'No, Vito!' she cried in fear of his wild temper.

But he released it by kissing her again, and after the first furious onslaught which left her breathless and gasping they were sweet, coaxing, wonderful, welcoming kisses, which made her want to kiss him back, and for the first time Jolanda knew what other women felt when he made love to them.

He did it properly, she mused dreamily, while her hands pushed valiantly at his broad shoulders in a futile attempt to stop him from taking her too far along the road to paradise.

'Jolanda,' he whispered into her ear, nibbling it, sliding his tongue delicately over the lobe. 'Bad. Beautiful. Beddable.'

A bolt of wanting quivered through her.

'Let me go, you brute,' she muttered hoarsely.

His kisses rained down on her upturned face, easing her sulky mouth, tempting it to respond. It took all her will-power not to. It took all her concentration to keep her body as stiff as a ramrod.

Because she longed to melt. Yearned with an unbearable ache to be his *cassata*, slowly dissolving into the heat of his body. Which was very hot, intensely passionate, highly aroused. She realised this with a sudden shock. He did want her. Desperately.

His hands roamed everywhere, drifting over her skin, which thrilled to his touch and bloomed beneath his fingers. Jolanda dearly wanted to surrender to sensation and see where it took her, to discover the mysteries of desire. But how could she? Vito played with women as a cat played with mice. They were brief entertainment value and nothing more, after the initial thrill of the kill. Her emotions couldn't take rejection.

'Will you take your repulsive hands off me?' she grated, misery lending savagery to her tone.

'Mmmm?' he asked, apparently bemused.

Jolanda glared at him. He'd never been bemused by any woman.

'Oh, stop using me to get what you want. Take me home,' she said coldly.

He frowned and lowered his eyes so that she couldn't see his expression.

'You mean you don't want to come to bed with me?' he asked slowly.

Astounded at his blatant nerve, Jolanda tried to hold back her anger. Sarcasm was a far better ploy where Vito was concerned. He was never wounded by anger alone.

'Bed?' she said coolly, giving a little laugh of scorn. 'Oh, you dear, old-fashioned thing! Is that where you take your women? No wonder you have so many one-night stands. My God, Vito! I can't even recall when I was last in bed with a man!'

That was true, at least. And it had the desired effect. Vito jumped up from her and she was able to swing her legs with studied elegance to the edge of the sun-lounger and stand up. She staggered a little and he made to help her but she shot him a look of hatred, only to be stunned by the ferocity of his expression. He looked close to losing control.

'How many men, Jolanda?' he grated.

'You think I keep count?' she asked, sounding astonished.

Vito drew in a sharp breath. 'One day we'll get together,' he said in a tight, biting voice. 'With our combined experience, it'll be quite a night.'

'Captain Hook meets the Crocodile? Don't threaten me with horror stories,' she said, smoothing down her dress with an outward composure. 'What a shame you succeeded in fascinating me by the decorated jetty, the hunt for the ice-cream and the prettily arranged flowers, only to lose my interest when we made body contact. It must be a new experience for you to come a poor second to a bunch of balloons.'

Vito's mouth twisted. She'd either set fire to his temper, or amused him enough to calm him down, and she wasn't sure what might happen. He was so unpredictable. Jolanda waited, her eyes lowered meekly. She was poised, ready to run for the gate in the wall.

'Home,' he said without expression, holding out his hand to her.

Her look of contempt made him take back the gesture of conciliation. He drove her back to her lonely home, let her in, switched on the hall light for her and turned on his heel to drive away into the night.

In a way, it might have been less traumatic if she had stayed to warm his bed. Because he had aroused her; taught her that it was his kisses she had always craved, and made her think about their childhood and the day she had almost become a woman.

CHAPTER THREE

IT HAD been the summer she became sixteen, and the day after the episode on the beach, when he'd emerged like a male Venus to tantalise her. From that moment, whenever he'd come near, he had set her heart beating at a fast, irregular pace.

She, Nick and her friends had been in Mallorca, courtesy of her father, who had flown them all to a large villa he owned in the north of the island. It had been a treat. And it had been a kind of apology for not being around on any of her previous holiday breaks that year. With her invalid mother now dead, she and Nick had often been left to their own devices during holiday breaks.

This particular summer, all she'd had was a phone message from her father, saying he was tied up on a business deal. Disappointed, she had covered up her sense of rejection and set about entertaining her friends with as much gaiety as she could summon up.

Vito's unannounced arrival had astounded her. After all, he'd raged out of the house in London like an erupting volcano five years earlier and they hadn't seen or heard anything from him since. Not one word. She still remembered the emotional impact of his leaving and the hot, sleepless nights as she and Nick cried themselves into exhaustion.

Now Vito had returned. Different. More sure of himself, generating a dangerous sexual menace which made her body ache—and which told her that he'd had experiences with women. But he'd virtually ignored her and had gone straight into a deep conversation with Nick, effectively separating him from his friends. Jolanda had seen that all the old magic was there, that Nick would cheerfully die for Vito.

His friends had seemed a little annoyed. She'd been livid.

She'd thought she ought to tell her father that Vito had turned up. Nick was in danger of corruption. Three times so far, her twin had tried to run away to join his hero. Jolanda had wavered and then decided that she'd wait. She'd wanted Vito to be there for her sixteenth birthday.

He'd see that she wasn't a child any more. When he looked at her in her new, expensive and curve-revealing dress, he'd think of her as a woman at last and take notice of her.

It hadn't occurred to her to consider what might happen next. All she'd wanted was his attention and admiration. Somewhere back in her subconscious there must have been a secret yearning to be kissed by him; perhaps even more. But Jolanda had learnt to live for the moment and not build her hopes on the future, and so she had made no serious plans about the outcome of her actions.

She'd run upstairs to try on her dress, to practise moving, posing, all to deafeningly loud pop music. Her head had tipped to one side and she had considered her reflection, pouting slightly and lifting her breasts provocatively. The music had been switched off abruptly.

'It'll slay the local Spaniards,' came Vito's cynical voice in the silence, as she turned to see who was there.

Her resentful eyes flashed daggers at him. Judging by his casual manner, her sexy image had made no impression at all.

'They're already slain,' she observed coolly.

'It doesn't take much,' he conceded, sitting on her bed in a proprietorial way.

Jolanda realised he wouldn't look so much at his ease if he thought of her as a woman. He was behaving as though she were his maiden aunt and they were on a number twenty-seven bus. Provoked, she experimented with undoing a few buttons and studying the effect in the mirror. It looked stunning to her. It would have Nick's friends paralytic with desire.

'All they need,' continued Vito, 'is a brief glimpse of flesh, a flirtatious glance... Does your father know you're wearing that, Jolanda?' He frowned, as she continued to see how far she had to go before he noticed anything.

'Not yet. If he comes to my party, then he'll see for himself,' she said, turning to see how low the back dipped. Very low. Not low enough for Vito, though, she thought sourly.

'No chance. His family comes second to his business deals. He's busy stitching up gullible clients in Paris,' said Vito sarcastically. 'He never misses an opportunity to swindle someone.'

'Get out,' she said, rattled by him. 'You're under his roof. If you don't have anything decent to say about him then you shouldn't be enjoying his hospitality.'

'Short of bringing my own sandwiches with me, it was unavoidable,' he drawled. 'I've stayed as short a time as possible. I came to say goodbye. And to warn you.'

'Goodbye? You've only just come——'

'I came to talk to Nick. Not for any other reason.'

'Oh,' she said, disappointed. 'So why are you bothering to talk to me?'

Of course he hadn't come to see her. Why should he? Of what interest could a kid sister be? Even her twin found her wanting. And all her friends could talk of nothing but Vito and kept asking her when they'd meet him.

'I want you to let Nick go. You're stifling him. He needs his own space. You've always been jealous, Jolanda, hating it when Nick has wanted to do things on his own, or with me. He can't always be following around your skirts.'

She bristled. 'He's at boarding school for most of the time. That's hardly——'

'You're tougher than he is, more dominant. Yet you use your femininity for your own purpose. You write to him, long, intimate letters, expecting him to confide in you. You lean on him.'

'He told you all that?' she gasped, mortified at her twin's betrayal of confidence. Nick was the only person she could be really open with. Was she to be left with no one?

'Nick tells me everything.'

'He had no right!' she wailed.

'No. But he had to. He's been at his wits' end. He needs someone to talk to, someone he can trust.'

'He has me!' Her unique tie with her brother was coming undone and it frightened her. 'He has me,' she repeated in a shaky voice.

'He knows that it would hurt you if he said he found you too clinging.'

'You don't seem to care.'

'Don't I? Jolanda...I know why you cling,' he said quietly. 'I want you to search back and remember the terror you had, as a small child, and to understand your own emotions. Maybe then you'll stop acting the hard sophisticate, which you're not. Your father has handled us all badly, but particularly you——'

'Out!' she said with a murderous look. 'Before I call the servants to throw you out. You're playing the same old record again and it's boring.'

'Have it your own way,' he said wearily, sounding quite defeated. That startled her.

'You're going back to Sicily?' she asked, trying to keep her glare going, when she wanted to beg him to stay. Her contrary feelings about Vito were confusing.

'Eventually.'

'When you've done a little business here? Father says you're mixed up in some illegal fiddles. That you're nothing but a gangster.'

'Does he?'

Standing there, looking a little forlorn, she racked her brains for something to rattle the urbane and unfeeling Vito a little more. She'd seen one chink in his armour. Maybe she'd find another, and learn who the real Vito Velardi was.

'Father told me——' She stopped, her teeth driving into her lower lip as she realised that it was something better left unsaid.

'Told you what?'

Vito hadn't moved, nor had his face altered, but his voice held a steely ring.

'Nothing,' she said, hanging her head. 'Forget it.'

'No.' He walked over to her and caught her arms in a tight grip, making her gasp. 'Tell me,' he grated. 'Tell me what he said.'

'You won't like it,' she muttered.

'I wasn't expecting to.'

She kept her eyes low. 'He said . . . he said that he regretted ever picking you up out of the gutter because . . .' She faltered, suddenly her taunt becoming ashes in her mouth. Strangely, this was hurting her as much as it must be hurting him. Her face showed her misery.

'Go on,' said Vito in an unemotional voice, his grip intensely cruel.

'Because he might have saved himself the trouble, since you'd returned to the gutter you came from,' she whispered, through her pain.

Vito released her and she took a few steps back, rubbing her arms, seeing that he didn't know he'd hurt her and was lost in his own private hell. Her heart wrenched. No one could help him. He'd locked himself away so successfully.

'You can't blame Father!' she cried. 'He did his best——'

'No,' interrupted Vito. 'He didn't adopt me out of the kindness of his heart. It was a gesture. A cold, calculated, political gesture.'

'That's taking cynicism too far!' she cried loyally.

'I was barely half alive,' he said, his eyes glowing at her in a frighteningly hypnotic way. The whole of her body stilled. 'In hospital. No bedding——'

'Lying on scrubbed planks. Hard ones, with splinters which . . .' Her voice died away. He was nodding. How had she known that? 'He was good and kind if he took you from that place,' she protested, the glazed look in her eyes disappearing.

Vito heaved a sigh. 'You refuse to remember. All right. But remember this: when Nick comes to Sicily, it isn't so much that he longs to join me, but that he wants to leave your father and you. Ask yourself why.'

She ran over to him and slammed her hand on the door as he opened it. It shut behind her and she barred the way with her body.

'Nick's leaving?' she cried in horror. 'Going to Sicily?'

'When he's old enough. I managed to persuade him to wait for two years. That's long enough for you both to change, and thus to keep him. He wanted to run away now, but I discouraged him.'

Jolanda clutched at his lapels. Panic ran through her body like quicksilver, blocking all sense.

'He can't leave me,' she moaned. 'We're twins! Father's hardly ever around these days. Nick is all I've got——'

'You have no one, Jolanda,' Vito said with quiet cruelty. 'Nobody ever owns anyone else. Lives are shared, not possessed. Listen to me.'

His hands tenderly held her shoulders, as the distraught Jolanda stared back at him, her world spinning to hell again. First her father had rejected her by finding business more interesting than her, then her adored adopted brother Vito. Her mother had died, and now Nick was also abandoning her. She couldn't bear it. Nothing would be left. She must have someone!

Vito had stopped talking and was frowning down at her half-buttoned dress. Jolanda's lashes dropped briefly to see the sun-tanned rise of her high young breasts filling her vision. They were pressed against his chest and pushed upwards; smooth, satiny and full, a deep cleavage making a dark line between them.

Slowly it dawned on her that the reason he was immobile, the reason that his hands were absently caressing her skin and that his breathing was harsh, was due to the fact that he found her sexy.

All she could think of was that she could persuade him to stay. And if he did, then so would Nick. They'd be one happy family. Maybe...

She pressed harder into his body.

'Vito,' she whispered in a broken voice.

'Don't be upset, sweetheart,' he said huskily, managing to drag his eyes away with an effort. 'You've had an odd life, I know. But you have to make the most of what you've got.'

'Oh, yes,' she said, her spiky lashes lifting to his dark eyes. 'I intend to.'

Her lips parted and her face grew sultry at the expression of raw desire in his eyes. And she pressed so tightly to his body, she could feel the rapid thudding of his heart and the hard swell of his need for her. While her hips pushed harder into him, in a kind of primitive reflex action, she was bedevilled by conflicting messages. Thrills. Apprehension.

The facts of life were clear to her. Nevertheless, it was the stories she'd heard that unnerved her. And the fear of losing that control which she'd painstakingly worked so hard to achieve. Men, it seemed, were capable of rendering a woman helpless, of making them do things they knew they shouldn't. Her friends had whispered so many secrets about their boyfriends and she wasn't sure what was true and what was false.

'Jolanda——'

Vito's voice sounded hoarse and Jolanda knew with a triumphant surge that she had power in her hands, in her body. She was different from her friends. They hadn't learnt to hide their emotions. Vito wouldn't have the upper hand in this situation, and she'd be able to control every second of it.

She let her supple body move against his and he flinched, catching hold of her arms roughly.

'Don't do that,' he growled. 'You don't know what you're up to. Enticing men shouldn't be a game.'

'I know,' she said in a throaty voice, lifting up her face to his. She'd make him stay, with promises, with kisses. 'I know all about it. I know what I'm doing. Kiss me, Vito!'

He looked hypnotised by her full mouth, his own lips drowsy.

'You can't know——'

'I can,' she smiled, knowing she must be sophisticated for a man like him. 'Everything.' She let her fingers trail up his tight, clenched jaw, watching the muscles work there. 'All there is to know.'

She was shutting her eyes, he had already let his yearning mouth move down, closer and closer to hers. Then he seemed to shudder and freeze. With a shocking curse on his lips, Vito pushed her away, his face fiercer than she'd ever seen it.

'You little whore!' he snarled. 'You have the morals of your mother!' Then he went white, his eyes horrified, as if he'd said something which he'd sworn never to let pass his lips. '*Gesù!* How could I say that? It's your fault! Your antics have goaded me into an indiscretion!'

'My fault? Vito, what do you mean?' Jolanda asked in low rage. 'How could you insult my mother? You, who always pretended to have affection for her——'

'I had affection for Lilly Docherty,' he bit, his eyes flashing dangerously. 'That's why your father never told me she was dead, why he never asked me to the funeral! It pleased him that I had to say goodbye to her privately; to a cold gravestone. I'll never forget that.'

She felt his pain, and wished her father hadn't taken such a cruel revenge. Then she remembered Vito's accusation and frowned at him.

'Then what did you mean?' she asked scornfully. 'Mother was an invalid most of her life! You can't mean that she——'

'I said that out of pure temper,' he muttered. 'I was furious with myself. I apologise.'

'Oh, no!' cried Jolanda. 'For once you've spoken the truth. Something's wrong. I know it. Tell me what it is! You can't leave me in this state!'

Reluctantly, Vito turned on her his cold and contemptuous eyes.

'It's something your father should tell you, not me.'

'For pity's sake!' she cried. 'I'm sixteen tomorrow! If Father isn't here, you have to tell me!'

As hard as granite, he studied her, as if calculating the advantages and disadvantages of doing as she begged.

'I don't see why you should remain in ignorance all your life. Sit down,' he said grimly. 'Wait there.'

He came back a few minutes later with a bottle of Spanish brandy and two glasses.

'You might need this. I certainly need some now,' he muttered, sitting down on her bed with her and pouring them both a drink. 'Nick knows. That's one of the reasons he wants to leave. Your father flung his birthright at him the last time he ran away and was brought back, when they caught him at Heathrow airport.'

Jolanda went cold inside. 'What birthright?' she whispered, her eyes huge. She had to be her father's daughter. She had to be.

'Stan and Lilly Docherty couldn't have children,' said Vito bluntly. 'Her heart was too weak. She longed for them with an obsessive passion. All *he* wanted to do was to carve out a business empire, preferably in other people's blood.'

Jolanda was too shocked to remonstrate with him. Her worst dream was coming true. 'Go on,' she mouthed.

'Stan adopted you both, for reasons I won't go into now, and a short time later he adopted me. You and Nick were three, I was ten. We came from the same village. Rocca, in Sicily.'

Jolanda's eyes were rounder still. 'I—I'm Italian?' she gasped.

'No,' frowned Vito. 'Never call anyone from Sicily an Italian. They'd see it as an insult. In any case, you're only half Sicilian. That's why you and Nick can pass as English and why neither of you have my dark skin.'

She felt very small suddenly, all her self-confidence and poise burst like a popped balloon.

'We weren't from the same family, then?'

Vito shook his head in denial. 'Different families.'

'Our names——' she said weakly.

'Nick is short for Nicolo, his real name. Yours should be pronounced as if it's Yolanda.'

He was looking at her very hard, checking the extent of her reaction. She felt stunned into silence. Her father wasn't hers. Her mother wasn't hers. Even her name wasn't hers.

'How long have you known?' she asked plaintively.

'All my life, of course.'

'You never said anything.'

'I've known since I was small how to keep a secret.'

'And Nick kept it a secret from me!' she said brokenly. It was the final betrayal of trust.

'He was ordered to. Stan Docherty thought there wasn't any point in resurrecting the past. He did it because he loved you, Jolanda, not to be deceitful.

You...you have something of a block about your earlier life.'

'Would I remember things that happened before I was three?' she frowned.

'Oh, yes. Nick does. Many things.'

It was a world of secrets. And she had been left out. Why couldn't she remember?

'You said . . . half Sicilian?'

He looked down on her forlorn face with a mixture of tenderness and pity, gathering her into his arms at her first sob.

'Poor Jolanda. On the eve of your birthday, to hear such devastating news! Yes,' he sighed, 'your real mother had strayed. She never said who your true father was, but, judging by your colouring, he could have been one of the occasional English visitors we have. She ended up getting married to the baker in Rocca, a man much older than she was, and with a temper like a rocket. He was always making wild accusations about people.'

'You know all this? You remember? You were only ten!'

'In Sicily, especially in Rocca, that is almost a man. I'd been doing a man's job for two years, working in the fields from dawn to dusk. You tend to grow up rather fast in a society like that.'

'Tell me about my mother,' she muttered.

'She was beautiful, with a face as sweet as the Madonna's. She worked in the bakery and, when her husband wasn't looking, would save the poorest children some of the broken pieces of crust to nibble.'

'She gave some to you?'

Vito's face darkened. 'No. I was forbidden by my father to enter.'

How sad, thought Jolanda. His father had despised her mother. What an irony!

'What happened to her? How did she die? And your father—— '

'I think that is something you must remember for yourself. Your memory has shut it out. It's no good having someone else tell you. It has to come back of its own accord.' He kissed her forehead. 'I'm sorry, Jolanda. Your adoptive father was adamant that you shouldn't be told.'

'Adoptive...oh, Vito! I can't call him that! I still think of him as my father.'

'Of course you do. There's no reason why you shouldn't go on seeing him like that.'

'It explains why he's lost interest in me. There's no blood tie. Why does no one love me?' she asked miserably, feeling unusually sorry for herself.

'Stan does, as far as he can ever love anyone. Nick loves you. You have many friends. I love you.'

'You're trying to placate me! How can you pretend you love me when you always argue with me?' she complained. 'Besides, Father has his work, Nick's leaving and you're not going to stay! Are you? Are you?'

Vito disentangled himself from her clinging arms.

'No. I'm leaving after your birthday,' he said quietly. 'I don't think it's wise for me to stay.'

'Why not?' she demanded.

'Because you're too aware of yourself,' he said. 'And there's something about our relationship that is dangerous.'

'I thought you liked danger,' she retorted.

'Not with sixteen-year-old nymphets,' he drawled. 'Even if they're sophisticated little madams.'

She tossed her head. 'We could have fun——'

'My God!' roared Vito. 'Are you this bold with all the boys who hang around you? Don't you have any respect for your reputation, or for your body?'

'What's the difference between me and you?' she countered. 'Why should men be able to play around and not women?'

'The difference, Jolanda, is one of age, and discernment. And, whether you like it or not, society condones some philandering in its men. Women always lose out, if they are promiscuous. I didn't make the rules of life. Don't blame me. I merely take advantage of them.'

'I hate men,' grated Jolanda. 'They want it all and they damn well get it all.'

'Don't swear! It——'

'You swear! And so shall I, if I want! I refuse to accept double standards! I refuse to be cast aside by men who find me redundant! I worshipped my father, and you, and Nick. Look where that's got me! Nothing but a broken heart!'

Vito reached out a sympathetic hand and Jolanda slapped it away, her eyes dark in her white face.

'No,' she whispered. 'You won't hurt me again, any of you. I'll be the one to do the hurting. I intend to enjoy life and treat it as men do. If Nick is leaving, I'll become my father's heir. I'll end up running the company with the ruthlessness of a man. Wait and see, Vito Velardi!'

He studied her for a long moment, his face grave.

'If you've ever loved me, Jolanda,' he said, in a rasp, 'do just one thing for me. Never give yourself to a man you don't love. Everything else, if you have to. Not that.'

She turned her back on him and listened with aching heart as he quietly left the room.

On the night of her sixteenth birthday, with Nick's friends left in the lurch by the girls as they pursued the indifferent and scowling Vito, she was brighter, wittier and more sparkling than she'd ever been in the whole of her life.

The boys were fascinated. The Spaniards were fascinated. Each dance brought her a new partner, eager to touch her, to hold her woman's body, flattered that she seemed to find their attentions so wonderful.

Vito watched, brooding, drinking. Eventually he disappeared and it was a while before he ever returned. His visits were short and always ended in quarrels. The last time had been awful, the whole house ringing with accusations and recriminations, leaving her father to rage around the building like a wounded bull.

Jolanda had been heartbroken to discover that she too was adopted. But she didn't cry ever again. Neither did she trust anyone. She pretended that it never happened, that she was the daughter of Stan and Lilly Docherty. And she built for herself a barrier that was impenetrable, diverting all her sexual desires to work, driving herself harder and harder, watching herself become hard and very successful. But intact.

Jolanda gave a huge sigh. Things could have been so different. In any of her subsequent meetings with Vito, the quarrels, and the fast, biting repartee, she could have surrendered to the undeniable sex appeal she felt for him.

Neither of them had risked the consequences, although several times he'd seemed hungry enough to need a woman, any woman, and she could have let him know she was available. She could have been one of Vito's cast-offs, doomed to a perpetual comparison of him and other men. And how would she know whether he was making love to her out of pity? He alone had been perceptive enough to see that she was hanging on to Nick because he was all she had in the world.

So, despite her need, she had kept her ache for him quiet. She knew nothing about the finer points of his ability as a lover apart from the lurid details which her friends had subsequently regaled her with. But she had the last laugh on them. They carried a torch for him all through their teenage years and beyond. Whereas she...

Jolanda smiled wryly. She'd shut doors to her sexuality to protect herself from the knowledge that she would walk to the ends of the earth for Vito, given half a chance. But her pride would never allow her insane vulnerability to show.

The next day at work after the party on the steamer, her phone didn't stop ringing. All her women friends, it transpired, had miraculously decided to give a party and were dying for her and Max to attend. And...they all would pause at that point, then give a nervous little laugh. And, they said, their breathlessness giving them away, did she have the address of that gorgeous, wicked man who'd stranded them up-river?

She was on the phone to one of them, her dainty Gucci shoes resignedly resting on her desk, when Vito wandered in, wearing one of his Italian summer suits. He looked quite unreasonably *edible*, she thought.

Jolanda stayed in her relaxed position and didn't even bother to show irritation with her secretary, who was shrugging her shoulders in a pantomime of perplexed astonishment in the doorway. Vito would have talked his way into Fort Knox.

'Oh, you mean the man dressed like a soap advert? Why not ask him yourself?' she said sweetly to her friend. 'He's here.' She held the phone out to Vito. 'One of your fans,' she said laconically. 'Doing deep-breathing exercises by now, I expect.'

His eyebrow lifted and his eyes automatically surveyed her long stockinged legs as he took the phone and arranged himself elegantly on her desk, carefully ensuring his immaculate beige trousers were clear of the biros strewn all over it by pushing them to one end. Jolanda smiled to herself. Vito was Italian through and through.

'Hello? Ann...? Oh, yes, the blonde egg-whisk hair and endless legs...' He laughed huskily. 'Mmm, I do. Every inch. Mole on the left shoulder...? Thought so.'

Jolanda sniffed. He never forgot a female body. He had a photographic memory. It must be getting a bit full by now, with all those overexposed pictures.

'Love to. Why not tonight? Nine o'clock...'

He snapped his fingers for a pencil. Jolanda ignored him haughtily. He lunged for a biro, searched for a blank page in her diary, finding one some months ahead, wrote down Ann's address and said goodbye to her.

Jolanda took the phone off the hook. It would be too much for his inflated ego if there were any more callers begging for his address while he was still in her office.

'Promising,' he said approvingly, neatly tearing off Ann's number.

'No, it's not.' With a casual lifting of her legs, she swung them to the floor and stood up, knowing how elegant she looked in her expensive narrow-waisted suit in soft, businesslike grey. 'What now?' she asked ungraciously, wondering why Vito was watching her gently massaging her aching back with such an intent look on his face. 'I'm very busy.'

'Back hurt?' he asked innocently.

'I'm surprised the pain isn't in the neck,' she snapped.

'I know,' he said sympathetically. 'It's wearisome, being a business tycoon: chatting to women friends——'

'Say what you've come to say and go,' she snapped.

Vito really did try her patience sometimes. She shuffled some papers and frowned at them pointedly.

'That busy? You didn't look rushed off your feet when I came in. They were up in the air, displaying the only sole you possess. Do you do all your business from a horizontal position?'

'About the same amount as you,' she answered drily.

'That much?' he marvelled, thrusting his hands in his pockets and strolling around her office, examining everything.

'Doing a survey?' she asked sarcastically.

'What? Oh, sorry!' He gave a small apologetic smile. 'Force of habit. You never know when you're going to take over a business, do you?'

'Yes, I do,' she said firmly. 'And so do you. So cut the fooling around. What do you want?'

'Wine, women, song. What do you want?'

'To know what brings you here. And don't say a London taxi-cab or any variation on that. It's too old a joke and I'm not in the mood.'

'Hmm. You do get agitated when I turn up, don't you?' he murmured. 'I gather you're reckoned to be one of the coldest, hardest businesswomen in the City. Odd how I manage to get under your skin, isn't it?'

'Not at all, since you're the most irritating person in the world. And now, Vito, your time's up. Go and play word games somewhere else.' Jolanda picked up her phone and buzzed her secretary. 'Mandy, get Security up here, would you? Three of their huskiest men will do.'

'Three husky men and me?' he asked in astonishment. 'That's going it, isn't it?'

'Four men,' Jolanda said to Mandy. 'I want to see this intruder fly like Tinkerbell.'

'Nick's ill,' said Vito abruptly.

Jolanda's eyes narrowed. 'Cancel that,' she said sharply to Mandy. She tried to stop her hand from shaking as she put the phone down.

'Angela might contact you,' continued Vito. 'His wife.'

'I know who Angela is,' muttered Jolanda, worried. It must be something serious for Vito to look so grim. 'What's wrong with him?'

'I don't want you to go to Sicily,' said Vito sombrely. 'I don't want you to see him.'

Jolanda stared in amazement, searching his implacable face.

'Why not? Is he infectious?'

Vito walked over to her window and stood with his back to her. She could have sworn that his shoulders seemed more slumped than usual. Alarm ran through her. Nick was ill and Vito was trying to prevent her from seeing him.

'Answer my questions,' she demanded hoarsely.

Without turning, Vito nodded. 'I don't know the full English name for what they think it is. Something like spondylitis. The joints of the spine are inflamed. It makes the backbone hard and inflexible. It's painful.'

Jolanda sat down, her legs too shaky to hold her up any longer. Vito was a rat. A callous rat.

'My God! You knew all that yesterday evening and you didn't tell me?' she seethed. 'You rattled me around London, flinging balloons and ice-cream and stupid treasure hunts in my lap, and all the time you were aware that I didn't know about Nick! You cruel, cold-hearted, insensitive bastard!'

'There's nothing you can do,' he said flatly. 'Nothing any of us can do. It's in the hands of the doctors and specialists.'

'You might have told me! How did it come on?' she said tightly. 'Is it . . . what is the diagnosis for the future? You damn well tell me, Vito!'

'Pains in his legs, then his back. When I found out, I sent him for blood tests and then he had X-rays. He's on anti-inflammatory drugs now.'

He paused. Jolanda sensed a wealth of meaning in that pause and she wanted to run up to him and shake him, to tell him to stop torturing her, but she knew she'd never make it across the floor.

'You have to tell me everything, I have a right to know. He's my twin,' she said in a low voice.

Vito whirled around, furious.

'What the hell do you care about him?' he growled. 'He's been in agony for six months and you didn't even know because of your stubborn refusal to see the truth and your stupid pride and your stupid devotion to your father——'

'Stop it!' she cried, goaded and taunted beyond control. 'Stop it, stop it, stop it!'

To her own surprise and his, she burst into tears, hopelessly miserable, angry and upset, twirling herself around in her chair so that her back was to him and he couldn't watch with those damnable hard unfeeling eyes of his.

'I don't want you setting foot in Sicily,' he grated, unaffected by her tears. 'You'll make him worse by getting him agitated.'

'I miss him!' she sobbed. 'I love him! I want my twin. this is a favour I ask of you. Help me to make peace with my brother.'

Behind her, she heard Vito's intake of breath and turned her tear-stained face to his. Immediately she recognised the look of open pain in his expression and the infinite sympathy he felt towards her.

'Oh, Vito,' she cried miserably, holding out her arms.

He came, slowly, uncertainly, and knelt beside her, then gently took her head in his hands and laid it against his shoulder. She wept copiously.

'It's a long time since we were this trusting with one another. 'Remember,' he said softly, 'how I held you in my arms that day you'd tried to climb the ash tree and fell?'

'You and Nick had gone up there to escape me,' she sniffled resentfully.

'No. I'd gone up there to test my skill, Nick had followed me as he always did. And you followed Nick because you were jealous.'

Jolanda dashed her hand across her eyes, not caring if she smudged her mascara. She'd been furious at Nick's dog-like devotion.

'I hated you.'

'I know. And what about the first time you were hurt?'

His voice had become barely discernible and Jolanda could feel the tension stretching way across the room as he waited for her answer.

She turned her head away but his hand cruelly brought it back and she was forced to look at him. But she stayed silent, blanking her mind.

'Remember. A sound like rumbling thunder. The sudden, terrifying darkness,' he said intently. 'And before. The love you bore Nick and your real mother——'

Tears began to stream down her face again. On top of her distress about Nick, he was heaping horrific images which she was trying desperately to escape. They were the stuff her nightmares were made of. How did he know that?

'Don't torture me!' she moaned. 'I don't remember any of it! God, I hate you! Leave me alone!'

Vito heaved a huge sigh and handed her his black handkerchief without another word, waiting while she reached for a mirror from her handbag and dabbed frantically at her make-up.

'Take me to Sicily,' she said shakily, applying a fresh coat of lipstick.

His expression didn't change. 'You'll hate it.'

'I'm not going to fall in love with the damn island,' she said, viciously screwing the lipstick back into its case. 'I'm going to see my brother. You don't know what it means, to feel a blood-tie with someone. How can you understand? You're self-sufficient. You need no one.'

Vito's eyes had narrowed at something again but she was too upset and engrossed in her own worries to ask what it was.

'What about your work?' he asked, waving at the piles of papers on her desk. 'The phone calls to your friends——'

'Don't be sarcastic. Nothing is more important than Nick at this moment,' she said vehemently. 'And if you won't take me, I'll make my own way there.'

With a proud tilt of his chin, Vito met her challenging look and gave in gracefully, as she'd known he must.

'I'll take you,' he said, not letting on how annoyed he must be to surrender to her wishes. 'I'd rather you were under my eye than travelling alone and getting into all sorts of trouble.'

'I'm surprised you care,' she snapped.

'I care about Nick's good name,' he said quietly. 'He's now the mayor of Rocca.'

'My God!' she exclaimed. 'I had no idea!'

'There's a lot you don't know, Jolanda. A great deal,' he said grimly. 'When do you want to go?'

'I have to talk to my father first,' she said. 'He'll have to find someone else to handle something I've been doing for him.'

'Let me know,' said Vito, handing her a card. 'Contact me any time.'

'Apart from late evenings?' she suggested sourly, remembering his date with Ann that night. They'd end up in bed together for sure. Ann was a real man-eater.

'I said any time. By the way, you don't mind if your secretary leaves early, do you? We have an early date.'

Jolanda drew in her breath ominously. 'Two in one evening?'

'No rules about numbers, are there?' he asked suavely.

'If there were, you'd break them,' she said tightly.

'I'll tell her you don't mind if she leaves soon,' he said, going to the door.

'No, you won't. If she's made a date with you, then more fool her. She'll leave when I've finished and not before. You'll just have to work faster to get both women into bed in the time available,' she said through her teeth.

Vito smiled. 'You really must watch that jealousy, you know.'

'No, Vito, it's pity. For Ann and Mandy. And me; I'll have to pick up the pieces, I suppose, and listen to a blow-by-blow account.'

His eyes narrowed. 'What gossips you women are!' he scorned, and Yolanda could tell he was annoyed to think his lovemaking would be discussed in detail. 'But surely you mean kiss by kiss, stroke by stroke——'

'Don't go on,' she snapped, the cruel cut of jealousy's knife slashing into her breast. 'I find it terminally boring to hear about your escapades. I'll be in touch.'

His lips quirked at her unfortunate choice of words. Jolanda picked up a paperweight and hurled it at him, hitting instead the closing door. She subsided angrily and tried to keep her mind on work. Apart from the worry of Nick's illness, the thought of travelling to Sicily filled her with a strange apprehension. Something terrible had happened there when she was a child, she was sure of that. And she didn't want to find out. If she went there, she might remember, and her life was difficult enough without having the past haunting her waking hours.

CHAPTER FOUR

SEVERAL days later, they landed in Palermo, the capital of Sicily. It had taken Jolanda some time to persuade her father that she had to see Nick. He was annoyed that she even contemplated abandoning the project he'd given her. She had been engaged on a rather secretive piece of lobbying: wining and dining a man from the European Investment Bank. The aim was to persuade him to speak up for Docherty Enterprises and to fund the purchase of a site in the depressed south-west. It could wait.

'Sorry we could only get to Palermo,' said Vito, picking up her case from the carousel. He'd travelled light, carrying nothing but a soft Vuitton overnight bag. And wearing a pale grey linen suit, with a casual shirt, and a stylish straw hat which had brought Heathrow to a standstill as everyone gawped to see who the film star was.

Only one luggage carousel was in operation. To Jolanda's eyes, Punta da Raisa looked a depressingly hick airport, after the facilities she was used to.

'What's the problem?' she asked wryly. 'Apart from the whole darn place being asleep and about a hundred years out of date?'

'It's adequate.'

Vito was stopped by a customs officer, who gestured to the soft bag. With a mildly resigned expression, as if his luggage was always searched, Vito produced the key and the man began to destroy the careful arrangement of his clothes. Jolanda was fascinated at the unexpected peek into Vito's private life.

She didn't learn much. There weren't any girlie magazines, or even girlie mementoes. Two lightweight summer suits, a number of immaculately pressed and folded shirts, hankies, all black of course, underwear...

The man unzipped a black leather washbag and proceeded to open every bottle and sniff suspiciously, putting the bottles on the table and not bothering to replace the caps. Delicious tantalising whiffs of the scent she associated with Vito drifted to her nostrils as the man did so. She glanced sideways.

Not by the movement of a muscle did Vito show whether he was annoyed or not. He waited patiently, his face blank.

The man abandoned the case and its now chaotic contents with a curt nod. Vito acknowledged it with a small, sardonic bow and the man stiffened.

'Do you two know each other?' she asked, as Vito quietly pushed everything back into the bag.

'Old enemies,' he said with a faint smile. 'He was taking his time searching through the underwear of a woman I was with and I made an interested observation about this. He's never forgotten. Sicilians forget nothing, forgive nothing.'

'How childish.'

'No. Passion and pride. We exercise a private justice on this island. We aid our family and friends, help settle each other's difficulties. It's a matter of self-respect that no insult goes unavenged.'

'Heavens,' she said. 'Judging by the way you behave, I'm sure you collect insults by the bucketful. You must have a busy life, avenging them all.'

His eyes twinkled at her. 'We'll collect the hire car and start fighting our way through the traffic. I hope your nerves are up to it.'

'I've driven in Rome,' she said dismissively. 'After that, any other kind of driving pales into insignificance.'

'Like to take the wheel, then?' he asked, challenging her.

She smiled. He'd be surprised by her skill. She was a marvellous driver. In fact, she rather enjoyed the cut and thrust of Italian driving; it gave her a chance to release some of her aggression and show a little bit of pizazz.

'Love to. You'll have to give me a while to get used to the gears and stuff like that, though,' she said innocently, hoping he'd be surprised when she coped so well.

But she didn't. Palermo left her shaking.

No one obeyed many of the rules—if there were any—and it was evidently cowardly to signal. If a car wanted to go somewhere, it just forged ahead, regardless of any traffic in its way. Any vehicle on the road might turn left, right, or even reverse at a ferocious speed, without any warning. It was the survival of whoever had the steeliest nerve, or perhaps the steeliest car.

Even pedestrians regarded the road as their inherited right, stepping into it without looking, and then not even having the decency to hurry, but strolling across as if there were no madly hooting drivers jammed up on either side.

'My God!' she cried. 'It's like driving around Brands Hatch the wrong way! They're all insane!'

'Want me to take over?' murmured Vito.

She shot him a venomous look. He was leaning back comfortably, not at all concerned by the noise and the chaos. People had parked with a total disregard for prohibited areas, and even in the middle of the road because they'd seen a friend and decided to stop and chat. Gifts, kisses and insults were exchanged with equal gusto from car to car, either when stationary or on the move.

Jolanda swerved around a number of cars which had been run up on to the pavement diagonally, tumbled in happy abandoned chaos as if a child had flung a set of Dinky toys there. These drivers were the good guys. Others hadn't even bothered to be that thoughtful, but had settled themselves at right angles to the road so that it had become a series of chicanes. She'd never seen so many cars or such terrible lack of consideration.

'Is this why you apologised to me for bringing me to Palermo? Because it's full of grown-up children pretending to drive?' she asked, viciously twisting the wheel.

She was trying to avoid a man taking his pony for a run. The fact that he happened to be sitting on a motor scooter and it was only his hand on the pony's mane that stopped the animal from bolting merely added to her amazement.

'Oh, no. It's just that it's almost dark and the airport is a long way from Rocca. It means we'll have to drive for some hours. Shall I take over?' he repeated.

'No,' she said grimly, determined to master the art of driving by the seat of her pants. 'What is the philosophy behind this kind of behaviour? Last one home's a cissy?'

He chuckled. 'When you live on an island which has been ravaged by volcanic eruptions and earthquakes,' he said, watching her intently, 'you put your faith in God and forge on ahead, hoping for the best.'

Jolanda banged her foot hard on the brakes as a policeman stepped into the road with only his imperiously raised hand acknowledging the presence of a few hundred cars hurtling towards him. She tensed her body, waiting for the jolt when a ton of metal piled into her.

'Relax,' smiled Vito. 'Their reflexes are quicker than yours.'

By the time they were on the open road, it was dark and Jolanda's nerves were in shreds. Her whole body ached from tension and a slight cramp affected her hands where they had been gripping the wheel so tightly. Palermo was an experience she didn't want to repeat again.

'I think I'll fly from Catania when I return. Or take the boat. Or walk across water,' she said grimly, flexing her fingers.

Vito chuckled. 'You coped brilliantly. What a cool head you have. Great nerves.'

Jolanda's heart swelled with his praise and then she became wary. He didn't praise people.

'What are you after?' she said ungraciously.

'Your body. What the hell do you think?' he said blandly. 'Turn off here.'

The bright lights and depressing suburbs gave way to an inky black and she realised they must be in the country. Deep country, with no human habitation, unless everyone had gone to bed now it was past ten o'clock.

'Not a lot of night-life, is there?' she observed.

'The place is dead,' he acknowledged. 'Michael Jackson couldn't make the summer season here.'

'I doubt anyone here has heard of him. What do people do for kicks?' she asked morosely.

'Oh, we do our embroidery and watch the wheat grow. At night the adult population devotes itself to making babies,' he said with a grin.

'I'm not struck on any of those activities,' she said wryly. 'What am I going to do after dark?'

'Become very frustrated, I should think.' He lifted a hand to stroke her neck and she shook her head irritably. 'Now that's where I could help you——'

'There's a barrier across the road,' she frowned, slowing down as the headlights picked out a red and white striped pole.

'You're changing the subject. We were talking about sex.'

'You were. I'm more interested in the barrier.'

'Allow me to break it down,' murmured Vito, pushing his hand through her hair.

Jolanda gritted her teeth and stopped herself from rolling her head in pleasure.

'I'm trying to decide which way to go,' she grated.

'I'm trying to direct you.'

'Is there nothing on your mind apart from proving your masculinity?' she asked tightly, the back of her neck tingling with the touch of his idly drifting fingers. 'What route do I take? With the car,' she added carefully.

'Drive through. Take no notice,' said Vito airily. 'They put up barricades all the time. It doesn't mean anything.'

'You must be mad,' she said, ignoring him and following the diversion sign.

'Hell,' breathed Vito.

And it was. Within half an hour, they didn't seem to have got very far. That was because the road was virtually unmade and she'd had to slow down considerably to avoid her head going through the roof when they hit one of the liberally scattered pot-holes.

'I can't take much more of this,' she said crossly.

'Neither can I,' growled Vito.

She shot him a wary glance and saw his eyes were fixed on her joggling breasts. He raised his lashes and beamed. Jolanda felt a spurt of ice-cold fury. He was teasing her.

She was about to complain, when the engine sput-
tered, coughed, jerked them forwards and then died.
They coasted to a halt. There was an awful, dense silence.

'Hadn't you better see what's wrong?' she said in an
ominous voice.

'Me? In this suit? What happened to equality? Aren't
you the driver?' he mocked.

She got out, slamming the door behind her and looked
at the engine, hoping to see something obviously wrong.
It was chilly and she kept shivering. Vito's head joined
hers and peered at the engine too in a companionable
way which irritated her because she could sense his bubbling sense of fun being firmly suppressed.

'You've run out of petrol,' he said, in a conversational tone.

'I've what?' she asked grimly.

'There's no petrol in the tank,' he said happily.

'Why didn't——?' She clamped her mouth shut. She
should have checked but she was so all-fired eager to
show him what a brilliant driver she was. 'You swine,'
she said pleasantly.

'Dark, isn't it?' he remarked with an annoying
cheerfulness.

Jolanda sighed. 'All right, clever. What do we do
now?'

'Freeze, I should think,' he said. 'Damn cold, isn't
it?'

Jolanda wasn't dressed for the great outdoors. She'd
brought a woollen jacket to fling over her summer dress,
but it wasn't enough in the brisk air.

'I hate this place,' she muttered grimly. 'How far are
we from anything vaguely civilised?'

'No idea. Never been down this road. Well, Jolanda,
are we going to spend the night in the car, or curled up

together under an olive tree, wrapped in each other's arms? Or perhaps walking along this road hoping we'll come across a friendly shepherd or a band of crazed bandits?'

She eyed him sourly and rubbed her aching back.

'Bandits?'

'Haven't you heard how lawless we are on this island?' he asked mildly.

'I wouldn't put it past you to arrange all this,' she muttered.

Vito spread out his hands to absolve himself of all blame.

'How?' he asked innocently. 'And why? How was I to know that you wouldn't drive straight through that barrier like any sane Sicilian——'

'Oh, I can't spend the whole freezing night tossing words about,' she said crossly. 'I'm going to get some sleep.'

By the time she reached the back door of the car, Vito was opening the door on the opposite side.

'We can't both sleep in the back,' she said coldly.

'My little *cassata*, I'm far too tall to go in the front. I'd never walk again.'

'Tough,' she said, clambering in.

He was quicker. They ended up in an undignified scramble and she seemed to be lying against his expansive chest and feeling much warmer suddenly. He hauled her around slightly and she had to admit that it was very comfortable.

'Let one hand stray, just one finger, and I'll eat it,' she threatened, too tired to fight.

'Now I know what a man-eater is,' he murmured into her hair.

His breath warmed her scalp and made it tingle.

'Go to sleep, you tirelessly evil man,' she muttered.

'I'll try.'

Jolanda must have fallen asleep almost immediately. But her dreams were terrible. It seemed that Vito was with her, but he was crushing the life out of her, and there was a roaring sound in her ears. She was screaming silently, and then woke up to find Vito cradling her, rocking her, murmuring gentle words which she seemed to recognise. But they were in Sicilian and she knew none of the language.

'Vito!' she cried in confusion.

'It's all right. I'm here,' he said softly in English. 'Do you often get bad dreams?'

'No,' she said, still shaking. 'Only rarely.'

'Always the same one?'

She nodded and he seemed satisfied. 'Come and see the dawn,' he said.

'Oh, my God!' muttered Jolanda. 'I've never seen dawn from this end of the day before.'

Vito laughed and they left the car, stretching their cramped limbs. He held out his hand, raising an eyebrow in unspoken query. Somehow, Jolanda wanted to stay close to him, to cling to his reassuring presence. She let him draw her into his body and they waited in the silence, leaning against the trunk of a tree.

In a slow transformation, like a dancer removing her seven veils, their surroundings showed more and more of their shape: trees, flowers, hills, all softly tinted in pink.

'The whore shows her face,' drawled Vito.

Shocked, Jolanda pulled away from him.

'It's lovely,' she said in a hard and condemning tone. 'But then you'd be cynical about anything just for effect.'

'No,' he muttered. 'I know it's all an illusion. That's my tragedy. Jolanda, sit down. I want to talk to you before we see Nick.'

'Why?' she asked, immediately concerned. She sat on the grass and he sprawled beside her, thoughtfully whirling the stem of a wild cornflower.

'I think you ought to be prepared for the way Nick is living.'

'Prepared for what? You said he's the mayor——'

'He's a pig-headed idealist,' growled Vito. 'Rocca is very poor and he won't live anywhere grander than the *pensione* that Angela runs, even though he could afford it. Or once could afford it. He's ploughed most of his money into the village.'

'That's so like Nick,' she said wistfully. 'It must give him a lot of pride to see the improvements he's responsible for.'

Vito gave her a jaundiced look. 'That's the trouble. His money has hit a bottomless well. He doesn't know how to wheel and deal, to scheme, to assert himself enough. His book learning has impressed the people but he has none of their wisdom when it comes to making things happen.'

'I could,' she said sharply. 'I could help Nick.'

Vito stiffened. His head slowly turned to see if she meant what she said. At that moment, she did. She wanted her twin to succeed, to show this supercilious man that they could do good if they tried. Suddenly it seemed a marvellous idea, to improve the village where they'd all been born.

'You . . . you want to help him?'

'Why not? I'm as hard-boiled as the best of them.'

Vito was silent.

'I agree with you there. But it wouldn't be fair,' he said eventually. 'You'd start to interfere and then leave.'

'I'd see it through. Nick and I will make our peace, and with father's contacts——'

'*No!*' roared Vito. 'He's not to be involved, I forbid it!' With an impatient groan, he turned his back to her and she had the feeling that he was more angry with himself, than with her. 'Don't shame Nick by making him think he can only manage if Stan Docherty pulls the strings,' he said tightly.

'There's more to your objection than that,' she said, alerted.

'Yes,' he said, turning a troubled face to her. 'If you get involved, you'll stay in Sicily.'

'What's wrong with that?'

'Apart from bringing the village to a shuddering standstill with your tight skirts and low-cut dresses,' he said drily, 'you'll drive me wild.'

'With desire?' she mocked in a pseudo-husky voice.

'Yes.'

Jolanda blinked. He was deadly serious. Her throat started to tighten up.

'Now what are you up to?' she asked calmly, disguising her trembling quaver with a cough.

In a sudden movement, she was pinned to the ground and Vito's dark and impassioned face was a matter of inches away from hers. She stared up at him with wide eyes.

'Stay at your peril,' he growled. 'I warn you, when a woman is elusive I find that exciting. I find you exciting. I want you,' he said roughly. His hand boldly curved around her breast. 'I want you here and now, in this hazelnut grove.'

The pain and the anger which his words evoked almost overwhelmed Jolanda. Vito wasn't even considering her feelings. He happened to be hungry, his strong sexual drive being unsatisfied, and so he was making his play for her.

'Don't be ridiculous. I'm not into country pastimes, like romping in the bushes. What is it about men that makes them so eager to start the day with sex?' she asked in a near-normal voice, pleased with her self-control that kept her face a mask.

Vito's eyes glittered. 'Something to do with body rhythms. Let me show you some of mine.'

'No, thank you. Not on an empty stomach,' she said in a disdainful tone.

Vito smiled. 'OK. On your back will do.'

With a cynical look, she suddenly arched her body to throw him off but he pushed her to the ground again, his hands gripping her upper arms and his weight trapping her.

'No, Jolanda. You won't escape me. We're stranded and might as well enjoy ourselves until someone passes by. What could be better than a little early morning sex? Or perhaps a lot?'

'With you?' she asked, wrinkling her nose. 'I could think of a thousand things which would be better. A little early morning trip to the executioner, a little early morning awakening by the KGB——'

Vito's hand reached up and touched her hair. It was a simple gesture. But he did it as if he was touching something beautiful and rare, his face transformed with awe, and it made her heart thump heavily.

'Leave me alone,' she said in a low warning.

'I can't,' he said simply. 'I thought I could. I was trying——' He let out an exasperated breath. 'I'm caught in my own trap.'

Jolanda, meeting his narrowed eyes, felt breathless. If she read him correctly, he'd been trying to manipulate her in some way and was finding himself unwillingly attracted. She could go one of two ways. But which? She knew the one she wanted. Oh, it was hard, being disciplined and sensible!

'Most lawless poachers are, eventually,' she said croakily, damning herself with her own voice.

Vito laughed shakily. His head bent to one side and he inhaled the scent of her hair. Jolanda trembled. His behaviour was disarming her. If he carried on like that, she'd have no defences left at all. She stared at him, panic-stricken. And she felt her lids half close at the primitive curl of his mouth. It spoke of sexual satisfaction. The very thought of that filled her aching, empty body with excitement.

'Let me tell you something about Sicilians,' he breathed, his face nuzzling her neck. 'About the way they learn at an early age to read eyes...'

She shut hers. And felt the slow lick of his tongue around the lobe of her ear. It sent her crazy. She let out a gasp as the tremors pulsed through her body.

'I'm not interested,' she said, her words flat with control.

'They look for hidden signs.' Vito's mouth fitted smoothly around her jawline and ran moistly upwards, his tongue teasing. Jolanda flinched in response. 'Slight gestures, which convey messages,' he whispered.

'My message isn't getting through to you,' she said jerkily.

'Yes, it is,' he muttered, plundering the smooth skin of her shoulder with his teeth.

'Vito,' she moaned, her longing and her long, lonely separation from him filling her heart.

'Jolanda.'

He said her name as if it were music. She gave him a yearning look from under her lashes, incapable of denying the truth.

'This is crazy,' she breathed.

'I know. We'll both regret it. But it's inevitable, isn't it?'

Jolanda felt nothing but pain and desire. She was dizzy with them both, the sharp thrusting knives repeatedly stabbing inside her, and she didn't know which of them were from pain and which were from desire.

His lips touched her throat and made her aware of the pulse that beat there insistently. Her hands clutched at his shoulders, and then one slid up into his black hair. Vito let out a harsh breath, and she saw from his savage expression that a volcano of emotion was ready to boil over, and she was afraid of his violence.

But it was a gentle torment as his lips tasted her skin, and one of his hands drifted with maddening delicacy of touch over the material of her dress and found her breast. She felt it flower and bud, agonising over the hot fever in her loins.

Unconsciously, she shifted her body to demand that he satisfy her other breast and Vito gave a sharp intake of breath when she writhed beneath him.

He raised himself slightly, looking down on her, his eyes dark with hunger. He watched her face, unsmiling, while he caressed her, circling her nipple till she was thrusting herself up to him, an expression of desperate pleading on her face. Swamped with desire, she couldn't speak for the need, but used her eyes, wantonly asking him to read what was in them.

He made a short, urgent sound in his throat and her head fell back as he met her demand and his forefinger began to rub the sensitive peak with a steady, unbearable rhythm. Her body began to respond.

Her hips rose in an involuntary movement, inviting him. She welcomed the sudden fierceness of his reaction, the way his body ground into hers, deliberately imprinting on her his powerful virility. She welcomed his impassioned kiss, thrilling to the black depths of his eyes as they slowly glazed in desire.

Her body shook with the intensity of her need, flames leaping within her, till every part of her seemed touched by his: lips, hands, arms, breasts, stomach, legs...

Her hands reached around his back and brought his hips harder into hers and she frantically tried to shift her body so that she could gain the most pleasure from the hard pillar that pressed into her.

'Jolanda,' came his faraway voice, thick with lust.

His hands tore open the buttons of her dress, parting it in a rough exultation which was so strong that she felt it too. For a while, he did nothing, except look and breathe.

'Damn you,' she whispered, her heart somersaulting at the expression on his face. He found her beautiful. He was aching, like her. Before her eyes, her breasts rose towards him, surrendering to his hands, his mouth, whatever he would offer to appease her.

'Damn you,' he agreed, his eyes briefly flickering to hers.

She watched his lips part and his tongue deliberately moisten them. Her lips had parted, too, in breathy sobs of anticipation.

With a tormenting slowness, he bent his head and Jolanda's whole body tensed, waiting. Suddenly his mouth was urgently searching the high curve of her breast. Then he encircled it completely, his lips warm and soft. Her hand caught a fistful of his hair and she drew him up slightly. Obediently, his tongue slithered over one unbearably tight nipple and she groaned in shock.

'Vito,' she choked, tossing her head from side to side as his mouth began to draw on it with an exquisite gentleness. Her body was so arched, it was like a bow beneath him. She was shameless, she thought in despair, unable to prevent her wanton response.

'Yes,' he whispered. 'Yes, yes, yes. All this time...' His mouth described an aching trail to her other breast. 'I've wanted you.' A caressing hand skilfully pushed up her skirt and Jolanda wriggled her legs to help, groaning at her own weak will. 'To feel your body beneath mine, the beating of your heart, to caress the nakedness of your beautiful breasts with my hands, my mouth, my tongue.'

'Please,' she moaned, shivering with the torture of it all.

'In my own good time,' he murmured, sliding his hand up her thigh, and she knew his withdrawal from her breast meant that he was watching her reactions, gauging her approval. Or perhaps it excited him, to see...

'Ohhhh!' Jolanda gave a long, deep shudder.

'There?' he asked in a hoarse voice.

She nodded wordlessly. There. Oh, God, she thought, just there. It was a sensation she'd never known. A fierce ecstasy brought about by the lightest touch, and she could no longer refuse him or deny him anything he asked for.

She would give him everything he wanted if only he would continue to touch her like that.

'Just there. Just like that...'

His mouth enclosed hers and she was swept into a whirlpool of sensation as he told her with his tongue what he wanted to do, as one hand teased her breast unmercifully and that damnable sweet and terrible rhythm flowed like hot quicksilver between her thighs.

'And more to come,' he promised.

'There,' she repeated mindlessly. 'Don't stop. Don't ever stop, Vito. Forever. Go on forever.'

'My God!' he breathed, sounding totally out of control. 'Sweetheart, we have to stop this.'

Giving the lie to his words, he kissed her repeatedly, with a desperate passion. But then she sensed it was because he'd decided for some cruel reason not to go on and he knew his lust would not be assuaged.

She would make him continue, she'd make him lose that damnable self-control. Hardly knowing what she was doing or what she was planning, Jolanda clung to him hard, reluctant to let him go. No man had aroused her this far. None had shaken her with such an intensity of feeling. He couldn't stop now. She had years of suppressed sex to make up for, and he'd brought it to the surface and taken her to the brink of surrender.

'No,' she said fiercely. 'No! You can't stop.'

'I know we want each other. Oh, God! Help me, Jolanda! Hell, I've been a fool——'

She caught his hand which had begun to move away from her thigh.

'No,' he said grimly. 'I won't let you seduce me from the path I've chosen.'

Her eyes opened wide and her mouth fell open. Vito closed his eyes in the pain of frustration and his teeth clenched. But not for long.

'I can't,' he breathed. 'God help me!'

In a dazed bewilderment at his swift change of mind, she watched his sultry arched lips descend to take hers in a long, bruising kiss that seemed to go on forever.

The pressure of his fingers as they skimmed her nipple became harder and she jerked with shock when his other hand moved with a rough disregard for her. And she recognised his utter desperation in that of her own.

Jolanda found her head was swimming with pleasure. She could no longer distinguish between the sensations, only that within her there was a wild feeling swelling up, higher and higher, flushing through every part of her body, rising to her head and rendering her incapable of rational thought.

'Oh, Vito, Vito!' she cried aloud, as his fingers sought to please her. 'Kiss me again, kiss me!'

'Oh, Jolanda,' he groaned. 'Why are you doing this to me?'

He kissed her, soft, sweet, with incredible deliberation. A tide of fire swept over her and she cried aloud at its intensity, jerking her body and bucking beneath his fingers, moaning with the wonderful sensation of it all. And yet empty.

The flames licked inside her, as she subsided and lay panting under his weight, Vito's head buried in her hair. He was still hard and unsatisfied. She wanted him within her and knew now what it was to feel real need. He'd taken the edge off her hunger, but that was all. Only one thing would really end her frustration.

And he'd aroused her, handled her with an insulting intimacy and kept himself distant from her. While his body and mouth were saying one thing, his mind remained his own: cunning, shrewd, assessing. She felt degraded and cheap. All he had done was to play with her, as if she were a toy. It galled her that she'd wanted him so much that she'd been incapable of stopping him, whereas he'd been in control all along.

She turned her head away from him.

'Bastard,' she whispered.

His body tensed. He caught her chin and cruelly turned it. His eyes were dark and hollowed in his white face.

'No,' he grated. 'Oh, no. Don't start pretending that it was all my fault. You wanted every bit of that and more,' he said with bitter bluntness. 'You knew how to arouse me, how to move, how to invite. You did your share of groaning and begging.'

She put her hands against his shoulders and glared with an injection of ice which came from the depths of her being. Somehow, she felt she would never feel warm again, would never risk that surrender of her open soul again. No man, she thought vehemently, would ever treat her with such scorn.

In the face of Jolanda's virulent hatred, Vito got the message and got up, tidying himself, his expression hard. Jolanda saw that his shirt was unbuttoned and his belt had gone. Had she done that? She couldn't remember. Being so much unaware of her own actions was embarrassing. Insanity must have struck.

She sat up and stonily pulled her dress into some semblance of decency, wondering how to handle this situation.

She shrugged as if he hadn't humiliated her at all. The throbbing heat pulsed violently in her loins, taunting her. That emptiness and frustration her friends had spoken of, and which she'd seen in their eyes when they looked at Vito, was suddenly something she was all too painfully aware of, too.

'I won't forget this,' she said in a flat voice.

'Neither will I. Not one second, not any of the sensations which came through my fingers from your body. Nor will I forget what you called me.'

'You know why I was annoyed with you,' she said, making it sound as though her real anger didn't exist. 'Still, it passed the time,' she added casually. 'Just as long as you don't read anything into what happened——'

'God! I could slap you!' he seethed.

'Why? For making the great Vito Velardi lose his cool?' she mocked. 'You did, once or twice.'

'It's not uncommon, when a man makes love,' he said grimly.

'Makes love?' she mocked. 'Oh, what a pretty phrase for something far more basic—or perhaps with more sinister undertones. And I do believe that you didn't always remember what you were supposed to be doing. That must annoy you. I know you pride yourself on never allowing your feelings to override judgement or the furtherance of your devious plans——'

'With good reason,' he muttered. 'I'm intent on self-preservation.'

'Try formaldehyde,' she suggested sarcastically.

'I think we'd better start walking along the road,' he said tightly. 'If you can, that is.'

'I'm not going anywhere. You are,' she grated, flushing that he knew her legs were wobbly. It meant that he'd reduced a number of women to jelly like this, and had helped them up afterwards. Hate him as she did, Jolanda didn't want to think of his hands pleasuring anyone else but her. 'I'm sitting in the car and waiting while you go to get petrol or a motorscooter or even a pushbike that will enable me to leave this God-forsaken place and reach my brother. After that, you can go to hell for all I care.'

'I thought this was it,' he said grimly, stalking away.

Jolanda waited until he'd gone and stumbled to the car. She hated the island. Hated everything about it. Hated Vito. His behaviour had effectively made her his chattel. Now he had power over her. All he had to do was to touch her and she'd be melting like wax in his hands.

It was the worst mistake she'd made in her life. Whatever he did, whatever he said, she *must not* trust him again. Surely she ought to know by now that he moved by stealth, in a manner so complex that no one could work out his goal?

He'd said he wanted her. She'd even protested that he hadn't meant it. Oh, God! How could she have forgotten all that so easily? She should have remembered he wasn't sincere, instead of half hoping he might be; instead of letting his lover's skill sweep her to shame.

Now he'd awoken her slumbering sensuality and it would be even more difficult to refuse him. But not impossible. She must find out what his real plans were, and denounce him for the fraud he was. Nick mustn't be mixed up in anything underhand, not now he was ill.

Her hand forced itself against her thudding heart, willing it to slow down. She refused to think about the warm, seeping languor which was trying to pervade her body. Instead, she sat bolt upright in the passenger seat, making herself invulnerable.

CHAPTER FIVE

IT WAS nearly two hours before he returned, in a ramshackle three-wheeled truck driven by a small, rugged man with a mass of tangled black hair. Sweltering in the morning heat, Jolanda noted with disbelief the farmer's thick serge trousers, his warm winter shirt and the cosy pullover. She knew he was a farmer because of the smell of pigs which came from the truck when it screeched to a dramatic halt with a burning of tyre rubber.

Vito slid from the truck with a vast polythene container in his grasp, paid the farmer what looked like a huge wad of notes, and walked a shade unsteadily to the car. Without a glance in her direction, he filled the car with petrol from the container which he gave back to the farmer and climbed into the driver's seat.

'You've been drinking,' she said with distaste, as he fiddled with the ignition. 'And it's not nine o'clock in the morning!'

'We had breakfast.'

'Breakfast! You've been drinking a distillery dry. I've been waiting for you all this time, and you calmly sit down to bacon and eggs and a barrel of booze?'

'Bread and honey. With beer. You want me to refuse hospitality?'

'When you have a woman waiting for you, yes,' she snapped.

'There's an answer to that,' he murmured, 'but I don't think you're in the mood to hear it.'

'Well, get the car going, then,' she said crossly, irritated with herself for causing him amusement.

'Don't nag,' he said quietly. 'You're not my wife.'

'Thank God.'

He turned to her with a face like stone.

'Look, Jolanda, let's forget it, shall we? For Nick's sake, let's keep up some kind of polite façade. Your antagonism towards me has always upset him.'

'My——!' She was lost for words.

For the past couple of hours, she'd been over and over what had happened, facing up to the humiliating fact that she wanted Vito and always had, and that he had taken advantage of that fact. She'd decided that the only way for her to cope with her shame and guilt was to pretend it meant nothing to her.

Otherwise he'd have a field day, knowing she was vulnerable. His vituperative, lashing tongue would wound her deeply if he was given the ammunition to mock her. Pretending to herself was even more important. If she could convince herself that she didn't care what had happened, then seeing him uncoiling his snake-charming powers on any other woman would never tear her apart.

She'd seen this happen to all her friends. He made good use of his short visits to their home and to his London flat. One by one, each one of her friends had confided in her that they were in love with Vito. Unwillingly, she'd borne the brunt of their confessions; how cleverly they'd waylaid him at parties, crept into his bedroom, or in one case stripped in his London office.

They'd described his lovemaking, which made him sound like a cross between Superman and a sweet-talking Don Juan. And then, eaten alive by jealousy, she'd noticed the signs of rejection as Vito the lover turned into a heartless Marquis de Sade. Her friends became pale and wan and usually a stone lighter.

Loving the feckless Vito had no future beyond offering a girl a foolproof way to diet, she thought wryly. It didn't do a lot for one's ego to be a briefly fluttering feather in his cap.

But now she knew how it could happen even to the most determined woman. At least if she agreed to remain on polite terms for Nick's sake, she might come out of this unsavoury episode with some dignity.

'OK,' she said grudgingly. 'Polite. And that doesn't mean laying me flat on my back every ten minutes,' she warned with a scowl.

'You should be so lucky. You won't have the time,' he drawled, starting the car and roaring off.

'Don't you Sicilians ever do anything by halves?' she complained, hastily doing up her seatbelt. 'A little gentle acceleration, perhaps? And what do you mean, I won't have time? I detect a nasty hint somewhere in those words.'

'Didn't I tell you?' he asked with suspect innocence. 'Angela is taking a break and visiting her family. You'll be running the *pensione*.'

Jolanda's mouth fell open. 'Oh, no, I won't,' she said, recovering.

'Then Nick has to. He needs whatever money he can get. I have my business to attend to. He'll have to stagger around and make the beds and cook the meals. It's that simple.'

'You scheming, conniving worm! You deliberately omitted to tell me!' she said in cold rage.

'Aren't we supposed to be polite to one another?' he murmured.

'In front of Nick. In private, I'm going to loathe you as much as I like,' she grated.

'Just because I didn't give you what you craved?'

Jolanda exploded with fury. 'Shut up!' she yelled forcibly, her whole body rigid in hatred. 'I'm tired of being the butt of your jokes, your sly innuendo, your mockery! Outwardly you look like a hot-blooded, sexy Italian. Underneath you're as cold and calculating as a computer in a ten-foot cube of pack ice. You take pleasure in goading me. All right, so you're better at taunts than I am. Is that anything to be proud of? Why do you hurt me? Does it give you a masculine kick to see me squirm? Do you like asserting your dominance over women by cutting them down to size? What's my sex ever done to you that you're so full of revenge?'

Vito didn't answer. He was staring intently at the road, his eyes narrowed, his jaw hard as a rock. She'd reached him, hit a raw nerve.

Something about the way he was holding his breath made Jolanda look at him more carefully, rather than burst into another tirade, demanding that he reply to her accusations.

His hands gripped the wheel so tightly that the knuckles stood out high and bone-white. His body shook slightly and she saw that the muscles beneath the cool lawn shirt were bunched and tense. Jolanda became alarmed.

'What is it, Vito?' she asked, puzzled.

He blinked and the tip of his tongue slid out to moisten his lips.

'If you want to live a normal life, don't ask,' he grated savagely.

Jolanda's body went cold. 'Are you threatening me?' she breathed.

There was a long pause. He flashed glittering eyes at her.

'Maybe.'

Jolanda kept her eyes riveted to his profile. There was a look about him which made her shiver. The skin on his face stretched tautly over the strong bones, reminding her of those gangster movies she'd seen.

A small prickle crept up the back of her neck as she stared at the withdrawn man beside her. He was peering at the road ahead through hard, narrowed eyes as if he wanted to murder someone.

'Do you know anything about the Sicilian Vespers?' he rasped.

'No.' Jolanda summoned up a normal voice with difficulty. 'Never heard of them.'

'In the thirteenth century, this island was occupied by the French,' said Vito in a low growl. 'On Easter Tuesday, at the hour of Vespers, a French officer searched a Sicilian bride, on her way to church. He inserted his hand in her blouse.'

'And?' breathed Jolanda.

'He was killed immediately. Within hours, every single Frenchman in Palermo had been murdered. Soon, in every Sicilian town, the French garrison had been thrown out or massacred.' Vito stole a glance at her. 'That, Jolanda, is what lies beneath the surface of every Sicilian. A private justice. An eye for an eye and a tooth for a tooth.'

The story had chilled her bones. Suddenly she remembered his cold-blooded revenge as a child; the story told to her by Nick. A master at school had unwisely imitated one of Vito's expressive gestures, and made the whole class laugh. Vito had sat calmly, according to Nick, smiling with the rest of them. And just as calmly had skipped prep and emptied one of the huge kitchen refuse bins all over the master's study. It had taken weeks for the stench of rotting meat and fish to go, and to remove the mashed potato from the carpet. Vito had told Nick that it was one of his expressive gestures.

There were other stories, and of course she had her own memories of how Vito always succeeded in getting the upper hand. She must never forget his heritage of passion. Sicily. Home of gangsters. Al Capone. Vendettas.

Now, he was intentionally letting her know that he meant to cause trouble for her. With Vito, that was not an empty threat. And the menace with which he succeeded in filling the air between them was real enough. In England, his temper had been legendary. Out here, where it was part of the temperament of the people to express their feelings strongly, Vito would have no curbs on anything he chose to do. Sobered by the thought, she subsided into her seat and morosely watched the countryside pass.

It was lovely, that she had to concede. They had risen high into the hills, the olive and almond groves giving way to rolling fields of corn interspersed with vast acres of red clover. An occasional whitewashed cottage with a lichen-encrusted roof appeared by the roadside, but there was little sign of people otherwise.

They climbed higher and higher and suddenly she could see Mount Etna. The volcano reared up like a hazy blue cone in the heat, its top streaked still with snow, and above it curved a weird boomerang-shaped cloud.

Around it, bleak and barren, rolled the mountainous lava fields. Jolanda shrank a little into her seat, finding the scene unnerving as she thought of the people who'd died in the many eruptions.

Vito. A dormant volcano, outwardly calm. Erupting, destroying everything in his path, leaving chaos and desolation. She swallowed and her hand rose to her throat as an unnamed misery overtook her.

'You want something to eat?' asked Vito in a hard tone, not taking his eyes off the road.

Yet he must have sensed her gesture. Jolanda mastered her voice.

'How far?'

'Up there.'

She followed the jerk of his head and blanched.

'That's Rocca?'

'Where you were born.' He was looking curiously at her now. 'Does it bring back any memories?'

'No,' she said shortly.

'You look horrified.'

'I am.' She studied the daunting rock which rose sheer from the valley floor in the midst of uninhabited countryside. 'I hadn't realised it was quite so high up, nor that it was so isolated. There can't be any other village for miles and miles.'

'Correct.'

'It doesn't look the kind of place anyone would want to visit. Who on earth stays at the inn?' she asked. 'Nick isn't going to make much money by renting rooms in a place like that.'

'There's a fine Norman castle—that castellated building, right on the edge—remnants of the old Norman walls and some priceless medieval mosaics. There's a trickle of tourists. Mainly English or Italian.'

'And where do you live? I can't imagine you in a backward place like Rocca.'

'Get this straight, Jolanda,' he frowned. 'It's not backward, it's different. The people aren't backward.

Sicilians are renowned for their intelligence. And I live with Nick.'

'Oh. So you're going to be under my feet,' she said, omitting to apologise for her thoughtless remark.

'Not if I can help it. I'd find it hard to appreciate your beauty from there.'

'You're being boring, Vito,' she said.

The car turned on to a narrow road which coiled itself backwards and forwards in an endless snaking hairpin between pale green eucalyptus woods. Nothing was on the road, apart from the occasional basking lizard, which strolled away from the car's wheels with as much disdain for wheeled traffic as the pedestrians in Palermo.

'Don't forget,' said Vito. 'Rocca isn't smart.'

Smart it wasn't. Jolanda's eyes widened as they came closer and she could see that the houses, which seemed to be growing from the solid rock itself, were decaying and peeling.

When they entered the village through a Norman arch in the walls, and the car bumped uncomfortably over its cobbled streets, it was to find the streets deserted, doorways boarded up, dust-laden shutters hanging off their hinges and balconies collapsing in a tangle of rusting ironwork.

'People don't live here, do they?' she whispered, appalled.

'Not here. It's been abandoned. See the red circles on the doorways? They mean the houses are unsafe. Tell me your impressions.'

'It's grim. Grey, grimy, dusty. I find it depressing,' she said slowly.

He'd tried to prepare her, but she hadn't quite expected this. There was an area which had become pure rubble, where medieval houses with their high courtyard walls had tumbled into ruins and become a sad wasteland. A street of beautiful, gracefully carved Georgian doorways and columned porches bore testimony to Rocca's former glory. But now they stood alone, leading nowhere.

'Any other observations?' he asked abruptly, turning into a small piazza.

Here, at least, there was some life—if you could call it life. A number of men in flat caps and well-worn suits sat chatting in the shade of trees. Two young women sat on hard chairs, embroidering tablecloths, their faces turned to the wall of the house. A few sorry-looking dogs scrounged for scraps and a woman in black toiled up some steep steps carrying a basket on her head.

'I don't like it,' she said flatly. 'I ought to, I suppose. I ought to feel some rush of warmth towards my home. But I don't. It's alien.'

'Not surprising,' he said, stopping the car in the middle of the street beneath a huge chestnut tree. 'You've been brought up in a large city all your life. This is another world. Come on.'

'Nick lives here?' she asked, looking around. There weren't any signs advertising the inn.

'No. But we can't drive any further. He's up near the castle and the church.'

'Won't the car be in the way here?' she frowned, as she got out hesitantly. All the men were openly staring.

'If anyone else comes, they can park behind me.'

Vito hoisted her case on to his shoulder and picked up his bag, leading the way towards a cobbled flight of steps.

'The men are talking about us,' she said in a low voice, catching up with Vito.

'Of course. They'll know who you are.'

'You've been gossiping again?' she rebuked.

'Am I the type?' he asked cynically. 'They'll have worked it out. You couldn't be my mistress because I'd never be such a damn fool as to bring her here. It's hardly the place for romance. You couldn't be my secretary because neither of us is carrying anything like a typewriter or a lap computer, and since you look a bit like Nick you must be his twin. They know he has one.'

'I didn't know I looked like him. People have always said how unalike we are,' she said, beginning to pant at the steep climb. The steps seemed never-ending, but Vito, even burdened with the cases, was hardly panting at all. He would be in the peak of health, she thought sourly.

'You have a certain look about the mouth and eyes,' said Vito. 'And the way you move. They're very observant; they'll have picked that up. And sometimes you can say the same things, and think the same things. It's uncanny. I remember as a child, going to each one of you in turn and you'd both quite independently give me the same answer, word for word. I found it quite fascinating. Here we are.'

They'd reached the top of the steps at last and were in a dark, narrow alley. At the end she could see a wrought-iron balcony, and Jolanda was pleased to see cascades of pink geraniums trailing from it, the first bit of colour in the whole darn village.

They went into the Pensione Rocca through a narrow doorway and it was a few moments before Jolanda could see in the dark hall.

'Want to freshen up, or see Nick?'

'I'd like to see him,' she said, feeling shaky inside.

'Don't look like that,' muttered Vito.

'Like what?' she asked in a small voice, trying to stop herself from bursting into tears. It wasn't like her, but the whole oppressive feeling about the place made her utterly miserable and terribly disappointed.

She'd hoped beyond hope that the town where she was born would prove to be beautiful, somewhere she could fall in love with. It had been more important to her than she thought. Valiantly she fought back her overwhelming unhappiness and depression. Vito's hands reached out and gently held her arms.

'Don't look as if you need a shoulder to weep on,' he said.

It was the very gentleness of his voice and the tender look in his eyes which were her undoing. Vito seemed to like her when she acted like a child. She supposed it gave him a sense of power, of superiority, and reminded him of those days when she was one of his adoring fans. Her misery prevented her from saying anything and she shook her head in dismay at the emotions which had crept to the surface.

With an exasperated sigh Vito cradled her in his arms, and she stood tensely in his embrace, trying not to give in. It was Nick who was ill, and she had to be strong. Especially if she was supposed to be running this wretched guest house.

'Hello.'

She jumped at the sound of a female voice and saw a slender young woman with blonde hair standing at the top of the stairs.

'I think I hear the voices. I am Angela. Oh, Jolanda, it is good for me to see you!'

To her surprise, Nick's wife clasped her by the hand and then kissed her soundly on both cheeks.

'Vito,' scolded Angela, letting herself be greeted fondly by Vito in the same way. 'You say Jolanda is beautiful.

Like a Venus. You not say she is your woman. Nick is to be happy, yes? Oh! *Madonna!*'

With a cry of dismay, she'd abandoned them both, running into the back of the house, from where came a loud splattering sound as if something was boiling over.

'I think we'd better go up and see Nick, don't you?' suggested Vito quietly.

'Then you can clear up the little misunderstanding,' said Jolanda grimly, starting up the stairs.

'You were in my arms, and it could be said we were gazing tenderly at one another,' he murmured.

Jolanda's back stiffened and she paused on the stairs, forgetting the effect it would have. Vito's body came to curve against hers and his hands automatically went around her waist. To her dismay, Angela had come back into the hall and witnessed the movement. Her face aflame, Jolanda wrenched herself from Vito's grasp and stormed on ahead.

'Nick?'

'In here! Jolanda! I'm in here!' came his joyous voice.

She flung open a door and found him sitting in an armchair beside an enormous bed. With a sob, she ran towards him and then stopped.

'I can't hug you, can I?' she asked anxiously.

'Try,' grinned Nick. 'But not too violently.'

'Oh, Nick,' she said brokenly, her voice muffled in his neck. 'I think I'm going to cry!'

'You'll ruin your make-up,' drawled Vito.

'Nick,' said Angela excitedly, 'Jolanda and Vito love each other. So much,' she laughed. 'They touch all the time! Wonderful, yes?'

Jolanda was about to correct her sister-in-law when she saw the loving, sentimental look on Nick's face as he gently pushed her away to smile fondly at her. And

then the way he looked at Vito, as if all his dreams had
come true. She bit her lip and tried to think of a way
to let his dreams down lightly.

'It had to be your sister, didn't it?' smiled Vito, his
gaze resting indulgently on the astonished Jolanda.
'When we saw each other again, well, we both knew we
were kindred spirits. It was like finding another half.
But you'd know all about that.'

'Vito, I——'

'So, Nick.' Vito moved forwards and took Jolanda's
arm in the kind of grip that told her he wasn't going to
stand for her denial. He flashed her a look which held
a warning and she shut her mouth. Perhaps he hadn't
told her about the severity of Nick's disability and
thought it best if her twin was made as happy as possible. 'How goes it?' he smiled.

Perhaps he imagined that, now he was in his own
country, he could act the macho male and make her do
whatever he wanted. Well, for Nick's sake, she'd keep
quiet. But Vito would be made aware of that fact, and
that it was up to him to straighten things out.

'OK. It's good to see you.'

Vito reached forwards to Nick and gripped his hand
warmly. The two men embraced like old friends. It
seemed that Nick had become more Sicilian than the
Sicilians, she mused. Had she lost him forever to Vito's
powerful influence?

'Tell me how you are?' she said to Nick, kneeling
beside him on the floor.

'Better for seeing you,' he smiled. 'Better today,
anyway. I think I might go for a walk later. Vito, would
you like to go with Angela and sort out your sleeping
arrangements?' His eyes shifted to Jolanda and back to
Vito questioningly.

'I'll keep my old room,' said Vito. 'But Angela and I will go and let you two chat. There's a lot of catching up to be done, I think.'

Jolanda, recovering from the idea of her brother subtly offering to put her in one of his double rooms with Vito, was grateful. She and Nick exchanged gossip about their friends and then he spoke optimistically about his illness.

'There are good days and bad,' he said. 'Sometimes I find it easy to move around, other times it hurts like hell.'

'Oh, Nick,' she cried, her face creased in anxiety. 'You must let me tell Father——'

'No!' he said, sitting up in alarm. 'He mustn't come here. And he mustn't know that Vito is here, either. Jolanda, you have to keep quiet. There are reasons.'

'You're mixed up in some scheme of Vito's, aren't you?' she frowned.

Nick put his hand on hers. 'We want to help the village. The people of Rocca want the derelict buildings renovated so they can move back from the new houses they were assigned. You wouldn't have seen it when you came up the south side of the mountain, but on the other side, below the castle, is a Government-built modern housing estate.'

'Surely that's better than being stuck up here——'

'Jolanda, this is a marvellous place!'

'You don't honestly like it?' she asked in surprise.

'It's my home. Angela's home. There's a simplicity of life which I am comfortable with. And I am useful at last. I can make my own contribution to the world. That gives me a good feeling.'

'And you intend to pluck people from the modern estate with all conveniences, and stick them back up here?'

'No one wanted to go there. They were compulsorily settled. It's an unsuitable site, marshy and unstable. Several times the houses have been flooded by the torrent.'

'Who was stupid enough to put the new village there, then?' she asked scornfully.

Nick withdrew his hand and stared at the sheet as if thinking.

'Corrupt businessmen,' he answered eventually.

Jolanda had the feeling that he was holding something back. She was about to question him when he spoke again.

'I thought you might have visited me before this,' he said gently.

She flushed. 'You hurt Father. I thought he was in for a heart attack, he was so worked up. I couldn't come here without betraying him. We work together, Nick.'

'Oh, yes. How did he react when you said you were coming? I hope it hasn't interfered with anything important you were in the middle of.'

'When I said you were ill, and he saw how upset I was, he could hardly stop me,' she said. 'I had to shelve a project for finding support for one of our sites from the European Investment Bank.'

'Sounds interesting. Tell me about it,' said Nick, fiddling with his signet ring intently.

'Father owns a plot of land in Cornwall. He wants to turn it into a leisure centre. I'm supposed to persuade the visiting official from the Bank Investigation Unit that it's a cause to plunge money into.'

Something about Nick's manner alerted her. He was shifting uncomfortably in the bed, and it wasn't anything to do with pain, but... She tried to fathom out what was going on and then felt a tension in the air.

Swivelling around, she saw Vito, standing in the doorway, watching them both.

'How long have you been there?' she asked fiercely.

'A while.'

'You overheard——'

'About your father's crooked scheme to defraud the Investment Bank, yes.'

'How dare you?' she breathed. 'Oh, Nick, I deserved better from you! You set me up, didn't you? I spoke in confidence to you. Vito, you can't discuss my father's plans with anyone——'

'Isn't it my duty to ensure that he doesn't bring unfair pressure to bear on the officials? Each project has to be assessed fairly, on its own merit. Bribery and corruption are serious offences.'

'None of that is involved——'

'Oh, I would have thought that sexual favours consisted of corrupting the poor official concerned,' he drawled.

'Sexual...' Jolanda's eyes flashed like splintered ice. 'I was merely supposed to be charming and take him around——'

'Show him the site, then show him the sights?' Vito suggested, running his insolent eyes up and down her body.

She jumped up. 'Nothing like that! I never intended——'

'It was your father's intention,' said Vito in a hard tone.

'How the hell would you know?' she challenged.

'Because he's done it before, several times, and used blackmail to sell his sites at a ridiculously inflated price to developers, who know the money will be largely funded by the European Bank. The only difference is

that he's not used his own adopted daughter before. He
must think you're every bit as good as the whores he's
employed in the past.'

'Vito!' rapped Nick.

Jolanda was so flabbergasted that she could hardly
believe what Vito had been saying. And then she gathered
her wits, trying to hold back the urge to fly at him and
tear her nails down his smug, supercilious face.

'You're jealous,' she scorned. 'You see how far my
father has risen and you compare his success to your
miserable little company, and you invent excuses to explain why he has business acumen and you haven't. If
you repeat what you've just said to anyone else, then
we'll sue you for slander and take every penny you have,
till you have to hock your flashy suits and go about in
rags. My God, Vito! You've always had it in for my
father. I hadn't realised until now just how much you
hate him!'

'So much for being polite to each other in front of
Nick,' murmured Vito.

'We can't stay polite to each other longer than a few
seconds,' she snapped. 'You always seek to infuriate me
one way or another. And getting at my father is despicable, after all he's done for you.'

'How blind are you?' he bit. 'Can't you see what he's
been doing all these years? Who the hell do you think
bought the site below the castle over twenty years ago?
What do you think your father was doing here, like the
vulture he is, soon after——' He stopped himself with
a frown. 'Ask Nick,' he growled. 'Ask him how the villagers were forced into houses they didn't want.'

Jolanda's head turned back to her brother. His eyes
were squeezed tight shut as if he was in pain. All her

anger for Vito dissolved as compassion for her twin flooded into her heart.

'Oh, Nick,' she moaned, holding his shaking hand within hers. 'We've upset you. I'm sorry. We shouldn't be quarrelling in front of you.'

'I'd rather you did that than carried on arguing behind my back,' he muttered. 'Jolanda, you must believe Vito. Father was in Sicily, trying to do some shady deal. The new housing estate is testimony to his success.'

'Perhaps he didn't know about the site. He could have been trying to help. After all,' she argued, 'he adopted us, didn't he? That was the gesture of a good man, someone with a sense of compassion and humanity. You can't deny that it took a generous man to pluck three orphans from a poor village in Sicily and give them a home.'

Nick was looking at Vito helplessly. 'Vito——' he began.

'Lunch is ready,' growled Vito, disappearing down the stairs.

Jolanda heaved an exasperated sigh. But whether Vito tried to elude her or not, she'd get to the bottom of this.

'You won't leave yet, will you?' asked Nick anxiously.

She smiled sadly at him. 'No. I think we three have to thrash things out.'

'You could help Rocca, Jolanda. You're clever enough to work your way through the red tape. My office is deluged with papers.'

'I don't speak the language.'

'I could interpret and you could advise. You were always sharper than me,' he grinned. 'I remember how you alone could match Vito, insult for insult, witticism for witticism.'

'I think I'd better go down for lunch,' she said gently, using one of Vito's ploys to escape answering.

Angela served up some fresh pasta with sardines, anchovies, pinenuts, wild fennel and onions. It was Jolanda's first taste of real pasta and she had two helpings. They ate in the tiny courtyard at the back of the house beneath a shady vine, and if Angela had heard the raised voices from Nick's bedroom she gave no sign, and they made small talk. Lashings of local wine made Jolanda sleepy. She felt every one of her limbs relax.

'Siesta time,' said Angela, looking tired.

'And I must unpack.' Rising with an effort, Jolanda helped Angela clear away and then went upstairs.

Somehow she knew Vito would take the opportunity to see her in private, and she wasn't surprised when there was a knock on her door.

'Come in, Vito,' she said, not turning around.

'If you want to leave, I can drive you to Palermo tonight,' he said.

Jolanda moved backwards and forwards from the bed to the wardrobe, hanging up her clothes.

'Why should I want to go?' she asked.

'Because you hate it here and because I'm a bastard to you.'

Helpfully, he held out a handful of frothy lace to her, his face deadpan.

'You can keep your hands off my undies,' she said crisply. 'Sorry, Vito. If you want me to go, then it makes me determined to stay. Nick has asked for my help.'

'It's not a good idea. He'll say he needs your skills. But he must succeed without you or your father, as I told you before.'

'But you said Nick couldn't manage on his own, that he wasn't hard enough. Implying that I was.'

'That's all in hand. Leave that to me.'

Her shrewd eyes assessed his bland expression.

'We're dancing to your tune again, aren't we?' she said thoughtfully. 'You're working it so that Nick thinks he's achieving miracles all on his own. You're ensuring that I don't stay and influence him unduly. For some reason, you're determined to work behind the scenes and do whatever you want to with this village development.' A thought struck her. 'I don't suppose you're planning on using your own company to do the work, are you?'

'My company is too small,' he said placidly.

'It is. But you could merge with another.' Her eyes flicked up to his. 'You're not thinking of taking over Nick's share of our construction business, are you?' she asked suspiciously.

'No. I'm not thinking of that.'

Jolanda wasn't sure. He seemed so determined to get rid of her and so pleased with himself. Why would the slick and sophisticated Vito Velardi hang around a simple village like Rocca? Why would he stay with Nick almost as if he was making himself indispensable?

'You're up to something, I know,' she accused.

He smiled. 'Yes. I am. And you're not going to stop me.'

Jolanda tipped up her chin, fixing him with a haughty look.

'We'll see about that,' she promised.

Vito's mouth twisted mockingly. 'You're dealing with a master of intrigue. I have the discipline and determination to carry out every one of my plans, whatever...' he paused, making her quiver with the menace in his expression '...and *whoever* gets in my way.'

CHAPTER SIX

SUDDENLY the room didn't seem warm any longer. A chill had settled in Jolanda's spine and it spread through her blood.

'You're threatening me again,' she husked.

Vito nodded silently, not breaking the tense air of danger.

'What would you do to me?' she asked boldly in a strained voice.

His sardonic contemplation of her made her nerves tingle with fear. It was as if she were an insect which had deigned to land on his lunch and he was idly considering ways of obliterating it.

'I think I would find a way that gave me the most pleasure,' he murmured.

Jolanda saw how sensual and predatory he looked suddenly. Inside her, a dozen pulses picked up his meaning and leapt with alarm. He meant to force her to submit sexually to him if she interfered in his plans—whatever they were.

'And which would give me the least enjoyment imaginable,' she said harshly.

His eyebrow raised in disbelief. 'No. It wouldn't. That's what would hurt you most,' he said laconically. 'That you were willing to contribute to your own fall.'

She picked up a vase threateningly and he fled. His laughter could be heard down the corridor. Jolanda heaved the ugly vase at the wall, satisfied as it shattered into scores of pieces. This wasn't going to be an easy ride by any means. If she was to vindicate her father's name and prove to Nick that Vito was wrong, then she'd have her work cut out.

She was too agitated to sleep during the siesta. When she found her thoughts were buzzing round and round her head, she went to sit in the gloomy reception-room, since it was too hot and oppressive outside.

Here it was cool, but she despaired of the poverty which surrounded her. The horsehair stuffing was poking out of the buttonback leather settee, on the wall above the telephone there was a cheap and stained print of a boy in a Cavalier's costume, and the shades on two vulgarly ornate lamp bases had lost some of their tassels and looked forlorn and tatty.

Nick must be very hard up. For a while she sat there, trying to read a book she'd bought at the airport, but she couldn't concentrate. Eventually she heard Vito's light, quick tread on the stairs and looked up to see him apparently refreshed and bursting with vitality. She glowered.

'Vito!' she said in a commanding tone.

'Correct. Full marks,' he mocked, striding to the door.

'Wait! I want to ask you a question!' she said, irritated and trying not to be. He wouldn't get under her skin. He wouldn't.

'Very well.'

He spun on his heel and faced her, a dark silhouette against the bright light beyond. To Jolanda, the width of his shoulders and the pose he'd adopted looked unnervingly menacing, and she wondered if she could handle him. He'd been a liar all his life. He'd been quietly taking his revenge ever since he was weaned.

'This place,' she said with a dismissive wave at the cheaply furnished foyer. 'It's awful. Why is Nick here?

He can't have spent all his money in connection with the village project.'

'He has. This is Angela's dowry. Nick has nothing. Besides, he is determined to live like the people of Rocca and gain their trust and respect.'

'By living like a pauper?' she asked in astonishment.

'That's the idea. There's a house in Lower Rocca which goes with the mayor's job but he won't take it. I told him that he'd only gain real respect once he started acting like a rich man, but he won't listen.'

'Nick has principles,' she said proudly.

'And little understanding of the Sicilians,' said Vito drily. 'They admire success. Oh, they think he's an honest man and have entrusted him with a job no one else wants to do. But watch the difference in reaction when he goes out, and when I do. They jump when I make a request. For Nick, they smile and raise their chins a centimetre.'

'What do you mean?' she frowned.

'Raising the chin? It means, "I know, but I'm not telling you".'

'They move fast for you because of your gangster connections,' she hazarded.

Vito smiled. 'Perhaps.'

And he'd gone, leaving Jolanda to fume and spend a couple of hours rereading pages of her book. It was at suppertime that Nick dropped a bombshell on her. She'd begged him to let her ask their father for help, certain that he'd known nothing about the unsuitability of the site at Lower Rocca and that he'd want to make amends for the mistake.

'If Stan Docherty sets one foot on Sicily,' said Vito mildly, 'he'll be lynched before the other foot lands.'

'By your men, I suppose,' she said tartly. 'Sometimes I wonder if you're still a child, Vito, playing cops and robbers. I think all these sinister threats are merely a means of making people afraid of you, so they do what you want.'

'Try it and see,' said Vito, the muscles of his face clenched. 'Nick, tell her about your arrival here.'

'It's true, Jolanda,' said Nick quietly. 'They hate the very name we bear. As I parked my hired car in the piazza, it was pelted with stones. When I got out, I was spat upon. They began to encircle me, and if it hadn't been for Vito's arrival I could have been badly beaten up. They operate on some kind of bush telegraph. How they knew who I was, I can't imagine.'

'Oh, I can,' said Jolanda, her eyes meeting Vito's. 'Nick, they didn't object when you courted Angela. They don't behave badly to you now. Was that Vito's doing? Is that why I wasn't stoned?'

'Of course,' said Nick impatiently. 'Jolanda, you must stop suspecting Vito of ulterior motives. He only has Rocca's best interests at heart.'

'Then he won't mind if you and I make a common decision for once, and decide to use our construction company to make a very reasonable, cost-cutting tender for the work here,' she said calmly.

There was an awkward silence, longer than she'd expected. Slowly her head swivelled from Nick to Angela and then to Vito, who was unconcernedly looking down on his plate, slicing his veal.

'What is it?' she asked, puzzled by the deathly hush. Why were they all holding their breath? 'What have I said?'

'Nothing,' said Nick hastily, vigorously attacking a mound of roast potatoes. 'Lovely, these, Angela——'

'Don't treat me like an idiot!' said Jolanda sharply. 'I repeat, what's wrong?'

Nick chewed his lip and met Vito's raised eyebrow with a shrug.

'I haven't got your ability to dissemble,' he said apologetically. 'Jolanda, I have to tell you that, because of my illness and the uncertainty of it, I've sold my share in the company to Vito.'

'You've *what*?' she cried aghast.

'Steady,' warned Vito.

'No, I damn well won't be steady! Nick, how could you?'

'I needed the money, for a start. He gave me a good price. Listen, Jolanda, he can do wonders with it. Even more, if you decide to sell your half to him too, and give him a clear run. He can combine the two companies and make enormous cost savings, perhaps even . . . well, he has one or two plans.'

'Oh,' said Jolanda, the truth dawning. He was up to some fiddle. 'I see.'

'That's a relief,' smiled Nick. 'Things couldn't have worked out better, could they?'

Both of them were rubbing their backs at the same time and in the same place. They laughed ruefully. Jolanda saw that the anxiety lines had been swept from his face and she didn't have the heart to tell him her thoughts. The battle would be between herself and Vito. She wouldn't involve Nick.

'They certainly couldn't,' she agreed cheerfully, knowing now where to direct her energies.

She forced a sweet smile in Vito's direction and bullied herself into finishing the meal, mutinously listening to the conversation which centred on Vito's ideas for the construction company she'd *thought* was owned by herself and Nick. Now it was to be a different partnership. Well, she'd see about that.

'Vito,' she said in honeyed tones, as the meal drew to a close. 'I think I've misjudged you. Will you forgive me?'

'I forgive anyone who apologises sincerely,' he said quietly.

Jolanda admired his answer. But she still loathed him.

'I'd like to walk up to the castle. Will you walk with me and show me the way? As a gesture of friendship? It would be far too romantic a spot for us to quarrel again, wouldn't it?' She lay her hand on his arm and gazed into his eyes.

'Unnervingly so,' he murmured, a mocking light in his eyes. 'We ought to help with the dishes first——'

'Vito! You are not being *simpatico*! No dishes tonight,' said Angela gently. 'Take Jolanda to see the moonlight. Where has your heart gone?'

He never had one, thought Jolanda bitterly. Other than the one stitched on his sleeve.

Vito wiped his mouth with his napkin and his dark eyes looked at her from under lowered brows.

'If that's what you want,' he said softly. 'You're not afraid of the dark?'

Her smile faded slightly. She was. Terribly, and he knew that; he'd often slipped into her room and re-lit her night-light when it had gone out and he'd heard her weeping with terror.

'Not if you're there,' she said.

'Well, there's a moon. A hunter's moon. Willing to risk that?'

She smiled. Judging by that sultry expression, he really thought she wanted a little romantic rendezvous with him, out in the darkness. He'd soon learn his mistake.

'Let's go and see if there are any hunters about, then,' she said huskily, taking Vito's proffered hand.

They strolled as if they were lovers along a street so narrow that the moonlight couldn't penetrate. In the pitch dark, Vito's strong arm curved firmly around her waist to help her on the big square cobbles. Wistfully she wondered if she would ever do this with a real lover, rather than with a conniving cheat.

Her head tipped to one side and she listened. In the distance she could hear laughter and music.

'Everyone's in the piazza,' said Vito, interpreting her gesture. 'For the *passagiata*.'

'What's that?'

'It's the evening parade. Men eye women, women eye each other's fashions, boys flirt from a distance with untouchable girls, old men and women admire babies and discuss ailments. It's a kind of daily party, where everyone in the village is family.'

'Real life soap opera,' she mused.

'In Sicily it's more intense, more vital and enjoyable than any soap,' he smiled. 'In most towns all over Italy, it's happening now. Whole streets close in the centre of cities, so it can take place. People finish work late, about seven or eight o'clock, and the chaos as they hurtle across the city before thoroughfares are closed has to be seen to be believed!'

She nodded, interested, and they ambled on in the warm night air, Jolanda still working out how far she would go to prove to Vito that he had made an implacable enemy who could play him at his own game.

'It's a superb castle,' she said, genuinely impressed.

The stone was the colour of rough white wine. Its vast castellated tower had been wrapped in iron bands, presumably to preserve it, since there were enormous zigzag cracks in it. Vito led her through the ruined courtyard and she peered down over the sheer precipice.

'How far up are we?'

'Nearly three thousand feet to that ledge. Then there's about five hundred feet before the valley floor is reached. Magnificent, isn't it?'

Some tiny lights twinkled, far below, and Jolanda realised that must be the new estate. It was like looking down from an aeroplane, they were so high.

'And now,' she said, pleasantly, preparing to enjoy herself.

'Now we take advantage of the privacy.' Vito's hand caressed her shoulder.

'Vito, tell me,' she said earnestly, as he turned her to face him. 'Whose idea was it for me to come to Sicily?'

He wrinkled his brow as if trying to remember. Jolanda wasn't fooled for a moment.

'Didn't you insist?' he asked innocently.

'Nick asked you to get me over here, didn't he?' She smiled, keeping her eyes down but toying provocatively with the buttons of his shirt. 'You only pretended you didn't want me to come, didn't you, knowing full well that I'd do the opposite of whatever you said? You are infuriatingly clever, Vito.'

Her voice had become husky. She hadn't meant it to, though it served her purpose. The trouble was, he'd gently pulled her into his hard, unyielding body and every inch of her was still patterned with memories of their recent lovemaking.

'What does it matter, as long as you're here with me?' he murmured, his head descending.

'Partners,' she said loudly, moving her head so that his kiss changed into a clumsy peck on her temple. That will have annoyed him, she thought maliciously. Not only did he fail to achieve his objective, but his customary smoothness failed for once. 'Do you realise we're partners? Was it your intention that Nick should persuade me to give up my half to you? Is that why you wanted me over here?'

'Jolanda——'

'Advise me. What shall we do with the company, Vito? Shall I sell to you?'

Vito had stiffened and she flicked up a flirty smile.

'What would you do with it, if it were yours?' she asked idly, undoing two of his buttons and pushing her hand inside his shirt. His chest was warm and firm, the soft rasp of hair slowing her fingers. Vito shuddered slightly and Jolanda tensed, finding his response and the feel of his body dangerously seductive to her senses.

The big chest beneath her fingers heaved with a deep breath.

'Whatever one usually does with construction companies. I don't play a daily role of any kind. I leave that side of things to my managing directors,' he said casually. 'My job is to sign the cheques.'

'You're not being honest with me,' she said, playfully wagging a finger at him.

'I'm not being dishonest. You must know by now that I don't discuss my plans with anyone.'

Jolanda thought rapidly. The only way to deal with a cunning animal was to set a trap. She ought to fight guile with guile. And she knew what to use for bait. The one thing Vito couldn't resist. His great weakness. Sex.

She gave a low, husky laugh. 'Not even with the woman who's hoping to share your bed?' she asked. Her heart began to thud loudly, the pulses below her ears deafening her.

Vito had stopped breathing. His whole body was frozen with shock. Jolanda didn't know whether she could go through with her plan. It was becoming too painful for her. For she'd decided to risk humiliation in order to call his bluff. She'd use all her wiles, every persuasive means at her disposal and get to the bottom of the reason for Vito Velardi's extraordinary manipulation of Nick. There was some vast and underhand plan beneath it all, she was convinced of that.

'I thought you said...'

His voice trailed away hoarsely as Jolanda plastered her body against his and languidly slid her palms over his chest and up to his shoulders. She stood on tiptoe and kissed his surprised mouth.

'Well,' she said softly, 'you and I might be here for a week or so. I don't know about you, but that's rather a long time for me to be without...' She decided to leave the rest unsaid, and gave him a pouting, meaningful look. It was amazing what one could do with one's eyes, she thought grimly to herself.

Still he didn't respond. Jolanda began to have serious doubts about her ability to succeed. She let her tongue slick along the outline of his lips and deep into the soft centre. His sharp intake of breath and the pressure of his big hands against her spine gave her an opportunity to let the tip of her tongue explore the soft inner parts of his mouth.

'Oh, Vito,' she whispered, shaken by her own actions. 'Don't you think we're made for each other?'

'Since the beginning of time,' he whispered, stroking her hair.

She'd done it, she thought triumphantly, hearing the tremor in his voice. Soon he'd be confiding in her and she could find out all she wanted to know. In addition, she'd have the pleasure of ditching him and letting him know what it was like to be rejected for a change. A kind of revenge on behalf of all her friends.

But strangely, the prospect didn't give her the pleasure she expected. And, as Vito's mouth dropped to claim hers in an intensely passionate kiss, she found it difficult to remember what she was supposed to be doing.

Having captured the elusive Vito, she'd need all her wits about her to hold him at bay. And herself. For his hands were roaming with increasing boldness and she was loving every minute.

Jolanda wondered if her Sicilian blood was beginning to flow in her veins, since she knew instinctively that tonight she mustn't make any obvious connection between her sexual overture to Vito and his future business plans.

Vito was a master at this game, and she a new apprentice. But he wasn't expecting her to be deceitful, and therefore she had the advantage. Jolanda quivered. Vito's hands were travelling slowly up her legs.

'Vito!' She looked around them warily.

'No one's here,' he said, 'only us and the nightingales and the moonlight.'

She suffered his ravening kiss. Suffered? It was all she could do to stay fully conscious. The more Vito kissed her, the more she liked it. Her mouth murmured softly against his.

'Not here, Vito,' she whispered.

'Where? In the valley below, beneath the olives?' His right hand had found her breast and Jolanda almost groaned her agreement. 'We could go down to the meadow and make love to the sound of the river running by and with the scent of the wild flowers all around us,' he suggested.

Jolanda put temptation behind her.

'I—I'm not a country girl, you must remember that,' she said shakily. 'I need somewhere civilised.'

'You turned down the bed *matrimoniale*,' he re-minded her. 'Shall I go back and arrange——?'

'No!' she said, alarmed. 'Not in Nick's house. I couldn't.'

'How soft your body is,' he murmured. 'Especially here. And here, it's firm. It smells of...' His head bent to find out. 'Jasmine. And it tastes of...' Jolanda's hands gripped his shoulders in anticipation. 'Hmm. Not sure.' He tried again, drawing the flesh beneath her collarbone into his mouth with a sweet passion that might have sent her demented if she hadn't hated and mistrusted him so much. 'Woman,' he growled, his eyes coming up to hers and glittering avidly. 'All woman.'

She couldn't speak. Vito's hand was caressing her head, curving into the shape of her scalp, and then both his hands pushed through her hair, and her head fell back in surrender to the wonderful sensation of abandon he was creating within her.

'My darling!' he breathed. 'Every bone in my body is melting. This is how I always imagined it to be; you and me. Alone in the darkness.'

She tensed, suspecting mockery. Vito frowned, then deliberately bent to devour her neck and throat, to run his mouth along the line of her collarbone and into its hollows. His breathing had increased its rate and she knew he would soon be unstoppable. So would she. She was on fire. Every inch of her ached to belong to him.

'No,' she moaned. 'I want it to be special. Not here.'

'Don't plan your life so cold-bloodedly,' he muttered. 'You wanted me in the grove early this morning. I can make you overcome your dislike for the outdoor life. What could be more romantic and exciting than to love one another beneath the stars? Think of it, Jolanda,' he urged in an impassioned tone. 'The moonlight turning our naked bodies to silver. The silence, the beauty, the passion. My passion. Yours.'

He was infinitely desirable. Jolanda gritted her teeth as panic surged within her. She didn't want to refuse. In fact, she couldn't reasonably refuse. Maybe at the last minute she could pretend to get cramp. That was, if she wanted to by then, she thought miserably.

Vito laughed gently and tried to push her to the ground but she resisted, her eyes dark with fear. Immediately, she saw an astonishing change in him; his teasing, almost *mocking* persuasion turning to open concern.

'It's Rocca, isn't it?' he asked quietly, his mouth suddenly serious instead of sensual. 'You're beginning to remember. Poor darling. Jolanda, I think in a while it'll all come back to you. I understand that you're confused.' His teeth snagged his lower lip briefly and she saw that he was trying to bring his passions under control. 'Shall we walk back?' he suggested. 'We can have a brandy with Nick and Angela.'

Jolanda raised her eyes to his and examined his face. He looked like a worried brother. It occurred to her that it seemed a natural role for him to take with her. Astonished that she'd escaped with her virtue intact, relieved and resentful, she nodded.

His arm draped in a friendly way around her shoulders. When they came to the alley, he stopped and took her in his arms, kissing her with such tenderness that she felt like crying.

'Don't be upset, sweetheart,' he breathed.

Her lashes fluttered to hide her huge eyes, moist with emotion. There was something eerie about the village, now everyone had gone indoors and it was silent. A shiver rippled through her body. Feeling that they were being watched, she glanced anxiously over each shoulder in turn. There was only the grim, medieval darkness.

'What is it about this place?' she asked in a wild, half-hysterical voice. 'Vito, what happened to me here?'

'It'll come,' he assured her, his lips brushing her forehead. 'It'll come.'

As they walked back, she worried that she had almost convinced herself he did care.

Over the next few days, she saw little of Vito. After a long phone call in the morning, he announced that he was flying to Luxembourg that afternoon.

'Don't look so disappointed, sweetheart,' he said to Jolanda.

She flushed. Her feelings must be more transparent than she'd thought. But her disappointment had come from not being able to prise some of his secrets from him. Not from the fact that she'd have to be touched by him again in order to do so. Jolanda felt a quiver of warm heat flow through her veins and grimly suppressed it.

'But I am,' she said innocently. 'There'll be no one to help serve at table when the guests start arriving.'

'Vito was banned from the dining-room long ago, when we first came here,' grinned Nick. 'Angela was very stern with him. I've never seen him so chastened. He would insist on overacting if any diners ordered him around.'

'You mean he lost his temper and thumped them?' smiled Jolanda.

'If only he had!' cried Nick fervently. 'No, he became incredibly *servile*, bowing and scraping, stumbling over furniture in a distraught manner, his hands shaking and conveniently slopping drinks over the culprits——'

'They stopped being bossy, though,' said Vito smugly, his eyes dancing with amusement.

'You very clever man,' laughed Angela.

'You're right. He is,' said Jolanda thoughtfully. 'Doubly clever, in fact. He's evaded a chore at the same time.'

'Oh, I loved being a waiter,' protested Vito. 'It gave me a chance to be a real ham.'

'I think the guests found me rather tame, after Vito's antics,' chuckled Nick. 'But then, any man is tame after him. I don't have to tell you, Jolanda, that he's exciting to be with.'

'Heavens!' she said rolling her eyes skywards. 'Don't flatter him. That straw hat is tight enough as it is. He'd be desolate if he couldn't strut around airports in it. Luxembourg must be given the opportunity to reel from the full onslaught of the Velardi sense of style.'

'I love it when you two fence with each other,' said Nick admiringly. 'And I'm so glad you've settled your differences. But you must learn the art of flattery if you're to live here and become Sicilian.'

Jolanda smiled weakly. Nick *was* pushing her, as Vito had warned. How could she let him know that she hated it here?

'I only give praise when necessary,' she said, a little stiffly.

'Vito, give Jolanda lessons,' said Angela.

'What in? She knows it all,' he said cynically, his upper lip curling.

'The flatter,' said Angela, not understanding his innuendo. She turned to Jolanda. 'He's good at flatter. It is lovely. It make you happy, give you smile.'

'We think it enhances life,' murmured Vito, gazing fondly into Jolanda's eyes. 'Flattery makes people feel desired, beautiful, more generous. We look at it differently; instead of seeing it as a rather contemptible method of crawling, we believe it is a means of giving happiness. So we praise the incredible beauty of a child and its mother beams on it in delight, the child responds with happiness. We say how marvellously young an elderly lady looks and she walks with a spring in her step and feels fitter than before. We even tell someone that never, never has anyone had such an appalling cold and how immensely brave they've been to make so little of it. It's fun and gives health and happiness to everyone. Extravagance is in our nature. It's in yours, somewhere,' he finished drily.

'I think not,' she said pleasantly. 'But it helps me to understand your behaviour better.'

'I'm so pleased,' he said, eyeing her suspiciously.

'Now I won't believe *anything* you tell me, rather than believe half of it,' she said, lifting her chin assertively.

Nick laughed. 'What price your sweet nothings now, Vito,' he taunted.

'They're not worth the paper they're printed on, by the sound of it,' he said ruefully, catching hold of Jolanda's hand and kissing the palm, his eyes twinkling at her as he did so.

'What a charming fraud you are,' she said languidly.

Nick seemed delighted to see the sparks flying between herself and Vito. And Jolanda had to admit that it was Vito who set the place humming with electricity, who made them all brighter. Especially Nick. Under Vito's encouragement, he was looking much better and spending more time out of bed.

That day, after an embarrassingly long and intimate farewell with Vito in full public gaze in the piazza, she and Angela went over the running of the *pensione*. With the help of a few travellers who arrived for a few days, her sister-in-law tried to show her how easy it was to run.

It might have been, if it hadn't been for the enervating heat, the unhelpful, suspicious attitude of the villagers and the fact that she spoke no Italian—let alone understood the heavy local dialect.

Besides that, the house lacked the facilities she was used to: a microwave, dishwasher and a deep freeze. She'd have to cook, properly cook, get her nails ruined washing up and shop daily.

When Angela finally left to visit her family, Jolanda was overwhelmed with a sense of inadequacy. All her life she'd coped brilliantly—apart from where Vito was concerned—and she wasn't used to being ignorant and helpless. At least the place was empty at the moment. No one had booked a room yet, but she dreaded the time when they did.

Worst of all, as she worked around the house, Nick kept up a running commentary on Vito, till she wondered just who this saint was who'd helped Nick so much. It was so irritating to listen to that she shut her ears to his glowing accounts and barely heard any of it.

The days slipped slowly by. Jolanda was working hard but felt utterly bored. Since Vito had taken the hire car and Angela was using Nick's, the village began to take on the aspect of a prison. Its limited size and lack of any facilities, its sleepiness and the dark, secretive people, combined to make her spirits plummet.

'Good God, Jolanda! What's happened to you?'

With a scowl, she continued to wash the marble floor, fully aware of the sight she must look, with her hair in wet rat's tails. She'd given up trying to use her hairdrier with the uncertain current. Besides, she'd fused all the lights twice.

'You look quite different without make-up. Innocent.' He laughed, as if that was a great joke.

Her hands rubbed viciously at the inoffensive marble. There was just a chance that her wishes would come true and Vito would slip and break his damn neck.

'Dumb as well as beautiful?' he murmured, closer behind her now. 'How lucky can I get?'

Slowly she dunked the cloth in the bucket in front of her. Vito's beautifully shod feet appeared by her right knee and she contemplated them for a few seconds, carefully. But she restrained herself. Then he pushed aside the bucket and was on all fours like her, smiling, meeting her, nose to nose.

'Hello,' he said amiably.

'Hello,' she answered huskily, and raised her hand, clutching the wet cloth, to thrust it into his face. But she wasn't quick enough; he caught her wrist in mid-air.

'Give the guests here that kind of reception, Jolanda, and they'll be wanting a cabaret every morning.'

Uncomprehendingly, she stared at him. His eyes drifted up over her shoulder.

'It's a local custom,' he explained to someone behind her.

Horrified, Jolanda realised he meant there were visitors in the hall. She jumped up, whirling around and wiping her hands on a grubby skirt, appalled at being caught in such a state. She wore no make-up and she looked *filthy*.

'How do you do?' she said, banking on cool politeness to overcome her defects. 'Welcome to *Pensione Rocca*. Have you come far?'

'Luxembourg. Came with Don Vito,' said one of the business-suited men crisply.

Damn *Don* Vito! 'I hope you had a good journey,' she said pleasantly.

'Oh, fine.' The man put down a small suitcase and she realised they intended to stay.

Damn Vito again! She was too tired and cross to find his actions amusing. Shopping every day and carting home heavy bags of fresh vegetables was no joke, especially when the water supply gave out every time she tried the shower. Nor was getting up at the crack of dawn for fresh bread. Nor was standing in the kitchen making pasta for Nick.

She moved with as much grace as possible to the reception desk.

'Single rooms for everyone?' she smiled brightly. Six of them! Could she cope? He might have telephoned!

'Please. And we'll all have breakfast.'

'Supper too, I hope,' suggested Vito.

I wonder, thought Jolanda, if he's telepathic? She tried sending some very rude insults in his direction but he kept giving her that silly smile.

'Wonderful,' beamed the man. 'We love Sicilian food. So spicy.'

'Good,' said Vito. 'Jolanda, when you've shown everyone to their rooms, perhaps you'd do us all a late breakfast in half an hour. We're starving.'

'Certainly,' she agreed with her sweetest smile. She refused to let him know he'd ruffled her. 'No problem.'

Hurtling down the steps to the square a few minutes later, she let her temper rip, muttering angrily to herself about inconsiderate men. She had to change some of her traveller's cheques at the grocer's and then dash over to the baker in the hope that he'd made a fresh batch of croissants.

Clutching the hot pastries and a loaf of bread in a paper bag, she toiled up the steps for the second time that morning, loathing Rocca and wishing Vito in hell.

The warm bread tantalised her nostrils with its orange scent. Baked from the hard maize which gave it a yellowy tinge, and which had made Sicily the larder of the civilised world in ancient times, the bread was still placed in communal ovens heated by the blazing branches of citrus trees.

Her mother had worked in the bakery. It upset her every time she went there and saw the baker and his wife feeding the fiery ovens, sweltering in the intense heat. Her mother must have had a reddened face and blistered hands. She must have risen before dawn and worked all day at the back-breaking job of pushing in the loaves on long slats of wood.

But she remembered nothing of this. Jolanda became moodier. She had to sort Vito out or she'd go mad in this place.

During breakfast, the men, their faces intent and sombre, discussed world topics, when she'd hoped they would talk business. She cleared the tables, washed up, did a few chores for Nick and ran down to the shops to buy food for supper, feeling very sullen and hard done by.

Even after supper, she couldn't settle down to wash up because Vito and the men kept her busy in the bar. Eventually, after midnight, she heard them going upstairs and made a coffee to revive herself, slumping in the chair and kicking off her shoes in exhaustion. Her respect for Angela had gone up several notches. She'd made it all seem so simple—and she'd had spare time for Nick, Vito and her as well. Jolanda felt guilty that she'd hardly spoken to Nick all day. He must be feeling pretty bored.

She looked up when Vito's bulk filled the doorway into the kitchen and noted crossly how his gaze toured the mess on the table and the dishes stacked up by the sink.

'Don't you say anything,' she muttered.

'How about "I'll clear this up and you have a drink, Jolanda",' he suggested, waving a half-empty bottle of wine at her.

'You don't look like my fairy godmother,' she said cautiously.

'My tutu's in the post.' Jolanda smiled slightly. 'That's better,' he said.

Vito poured out an enormous glass of rich red wine for her and she curled up wearily in the chair, nursing it.

'Domestic life isn't for you, then,' he observed, rapidly clearing the table and sweeping a huge pile of strawberry husks into the bin.

'You can't call it life! Running around after a gang of men isn't my idea of living.'

He made no comment. She watched Vito roll his sleeves up and run a bowl of sudsy water. He probably thought she was a spoiled city girl, incapable of a day's hard work, but at the moment she didn't care.

'I told Nick it would be a mistake,' said Vito.

All she could see of him was his broad back, the muscles shifting beneath the thin shirt as he worked on the saucepan she'd left encrusted with a cheesy sauce.

'You were right,' she said listlessly.

'Not going to fight me, Jolanda?' he asked, smiling over his shoulder. When she shook her head, dispirited, he left the washing up, wiped his hands on a towel and squatted down on his haunches in front of her.

'I've made arrangements for Nick to go to a clinic next week,' he said, his dark eyes serious. 'Nothing to get alarmed about, but it's a good time for him to try a small operation which might help his mobility. He'll be in for about ten days.'

'Poor Nick.' She frowned. 'Poor me, too! I'll have to stay here and run this place.'

'No,' he said gently. 'Nick's been worried about you. He thinks it's unfair to expect someone like you to adapt to the conditions in Rocca.'

'I tried——'

'I know. You must have been working hard, to neglect your appearance.'

'Are you being funny at my expense?' she asked suspiciously.

'No. We admire the way you look.' He took hold of her hand and examined it, then smiled up at her. 'I don't like to see your nail polish chipped and your hands rough and red.'

'How like a man! You want me to be whore and Madonna, seductive and domesticated, alluring at night, yet turning out endless pasta and cleaning bathrooms without getting a hair out of place!' she said waspishly.

'Hell, Jolanda, anything I say is going to be wrong, isn't it? I'm trying to tell you that I appreciate how well you dress and present yourself. I'd rather you didn't waste your talents around the house.'

'Because you think my talents lie in bed?' She glared.

He shrugged. 'How do I know? The evidence is thin, so far. No, I wasn't thinking of that, only that you were a round peg in a square hole. Nick says you've been incredibly committed to running this place but he's hated seeing you so miserable. You don't give in easily, do you?'

'I didn't have much choice, remember? You left me in this God-forsaken village. If I'd known, I would have brought my own entertainment. A four-piece band, a radio and half a dozen gigolos.'

'You could have hired a housekeeper from the village,' said Vito.

Jolanda stared at him in dismay. The thought had never occurred to her! 'Would she have amused me?' she asked, covering up her irritation with herself.

'Not as much as the gigolos. Jolanda, Nick and I have talked things over. He thought you might enjoy a trip to Taormina when he goes into the clinic. It's the kind of place you'd like.'

'You mean it has pavements and sophisticated restaurants and people who smile and electrical equipment that works and real water and the place isn't grey all over?'

Vito laughed. 'Poor Rocca. I can see you won't want to return.'

'I didn't say that,' she said hastily. 'Don't put words in my mouth. I'll do anything if I have to.'

'You're very tough, I'll grant you that. But why don't we have a break, both of us?'

'You're coming too?' she frowned. 'I thought this was a coach trip or something.'

'Or something. You've been invited to stay at a *palazzo* by *Il Principe*.'

'A palace?' She sat upright, pleased. Her eyes shone with relief. Civilisation at last. 'What do I call this man? How did I get an invitation?'

Vito smiled. 'You can call him "Highness". Titles are abolished, but everyone uses them as a matter of courtesy and . . .' He smiled again. 'Flattery. Nick wangled the invitation. Well?'

'Can't wait,' she said fervently. 'Can I boot out your friends tomorrow?'

'Stick it out for a week. Then they'll be gone and we close down.'

'Nick will lose money,' she said slowly. 'Perhaps I ought to keep the inn going.'

'I'm pleased you should think of him above your own needs. No, Jolanda. My business friends are on expenses. They'll pay hotel rates just to be here, close to where they want to be.'

Jolanda was about to ask why on earth the men should want to be in Rocca, when they could be in a decent hotel. But then she realised that they must be part of Vito's plans. She brightened up. If she hung around, she might find out what was going on.

'You can count on me,' she said firmly.

'I knew I could,' murmured Vito. A broad smile spread over his face. 'I knew I could.'

CHAPTER SEVEN

KNOWING that she was going on a trip and might even be able to wear some of the smarter clothes she'd mistakenly packed cheered Jolanda up immensely.

Either she was invigorated by the thought of escaping from Rocca, or she was becoming more efficient. There was actually time to spare, precious, wonderful leisure time, which she spent with Nick. He was improving daily, and that added to her high spirits.

One morning, she had an hour to spare before she tackled the lunch, but Nick was sleeping on the balcony in the sunshine. It was then that she saw Vito and the six men walking purposefully up to the castle.

Naturally, she followed. They were leaning over a parapet, looking down on the site of Lower Rocca. She crept as close as she dared and listened unashamedly.

'The dam would hardly intrude,' Vito was saying, pointing to the head of the valley.

'I see no reason why it can't go ahead, Don Vito,' said one of the men. 'Now we have all the facts. What about the bribe?'

Jolanda tensed expectantly, her eyes widening.

'I've arranged that. The bribe is already in hand and the first payment will be in Taormina. A nice fat one. Juicy, you might say.'

The men all roared with laughter. Jolanda, crouching behind a stone wall, felt surprisingly miserable. She'd discovered Vito's treachery, his crooked deal, and yet it

144

had made her unhappy to have her suspicions about him confirmed.

The sound of children's chatter intruded on her thoughts and she turned to see a group entering the castle gate. She pretended to be doing up her shoe, but the class hardly noticed her, the twenty or so children in all assorted sizes solemnly walking hand in hand in pairs, and heading for the open grass beyond the men.

The teacher began to organise a game, and the men watched indulgently, leaning against the wall near Jolanda, all business momentarily forgotten.

As the children began to circle a small, five-year-old girl with long glossy plaits, Jolanda caught the look on Vito's face and her heart gave a violent jolt. It was a look of adoration, of love, a sentimental affection that was incongruous under the circumstances and contrasted oddly with his evil business intentions. Inside her head, it seemed that a mist was swirling, and through it, she saw that look of his again, but on the face of a younger Vito.

And then it was gone. Shaken, Jolanda wondered if she should slip away before she was discovered.

'Does Nick know?' asked one of the men.

Jolanda hesitated, holding her breath.

'Nothing of this. I daren't trust him, or his sister,' said Vito.

'Surely he rejected Docherty and all he stood for.'

Vito grunted. 'That was my personal revenge, to take Nick from him, and all the sweeter because Nick didn't come to join me in the heat of anger, but after two years of considering the idea. *This* matter is my *public* revenge. But no one else is to know. If we're caught before the bribe is taken...'

The men murmured in agreement and Jolanda saw they were making a move. She scurried away, running like the wind down to the house. Taormina. It was to happen there. She must stick to Vito like a leech. Who could she talk to? Nick? Her feet slowed. They dragged up the stairs to his room and there her hand hesitated.

Not yet. She'd need more proof than hearsay. At the moment, she couldn't burden Nick with the information. Though she'd rifle Vito's room, the moment she could.

She was still standing on the landing, petrified with fear, when the men came into the house and she fled into her own room. If Vito was involved in some bribery and corruption concerned with building a dam, then there would be big money involved and she'd be in serious trouble if he discovered her interference.

How serious? How much of Vito's sinister reputation was deserved? Jolanda felt a shiver run down her back. But she felt more alive and vital than she had for a long time. Danger could be exciting.

She would search Vito's room. It had always been locked. She'd never cleaned in there. It seemed there was only one way she could get in.

That night, when everyone had gone to bed, she brushed her hair carefully, slid into a satin nightdress and oyster satin wrap, and tiptoed to Vito's room.

The key turned in the door as he unlocked it and he stood in the glow of candle-light, still dressed, his shirt sleeves rolled up to display brawny arms. Jolanda took one look at those brawny arms and gulped, thinking of the physical harm he could do to her.

'You look frightened. What's the matter?' asked Vito.

'I am frightened,' she admitted, knowing how enormous her eyes must be.

'Jolanda!' He pulled her into the room and she saw briefly a table covered in papers before Vito's hand was touching her face gently and she had to switch her gaze. 'Tell me what frightens you.'

She wondered wryly what he'd say if she told him the truth, that she was frightened of him.

'I can't say. But . . . I had to come to you.'

Vito drew her down to sit on his bed. Idly she let her eyes drift to the table with its scattered documents. Faking, she put her hand to her forehead and groaned.

'Can you get me a drink? Some brandy, maybe?' she asked weakly. All was fair in love and war, and this was war.

'Yes. I . . .'

Vito glanced at the table, evidently torn between leaving immediately and gathering up all the evidence of his double-dealing. Jolanda promptly curled up like a kitten on his bed with her back to the table and she heard the satisfactory sound of Vito leaving the room and his footsteps on the marble steps.

Instantly she uncurled and scanned the papers. Most were in Italian, some in French. Her eyes rested on a file, headed European Investment Projects. With trembling fingers, she opened it. Inside the front cover was a list for the current year. Two projects were competing with each other for a loan from the European Bank.

Her father's site in the south-west of England which she'd been working on, and the dam at Rocca.

Her mind raced, trying to think of the implications. Vito's steps came closer. Feeling sick, she hurled herself on the bed and curled up again into a ball.

'Brandy, sweetheart,' murmured his voice.

When she sat up, she felt really groggy, and dutifully drank from the glass he held.

'Thank you,' she whispered.

'I wish I could help,' he said quietly.

She raised pleading eyes to his. 'You could.'

'Tell me how and I will.'

'I wish you meant that,' she said bitterly, feeling the misery well up in her throat. Vito meant to ruin her father—and herself in the process. Only she could stop him.

'I mean it,' he said firmly. 'Jolanda, you have an odd idea of what I am. You don't know half of it. Yet.'

'That sounds like a threat,' she said shakily.

'No, it's a promise that one day you'll understand my actions even if you can't excuse them.'

'Then make your peace with my father!' she cried hotly. 'Stop hurting me through him! He picked you out of the gutter——'

'Don't repeat things he's told you!' growled Vito. 'I wasn't in the gutter.'

'You had no parents, nowhere to live, you were in rags. Deny that if you can!'

He passed a hand through his hair, leaving it tousled. 'I can't deny that,' he muttered, then fixed her with burning eyes. 'I can't forget his treatment.'

'Then we are enemies,' she said unhappily, her eyes moist with unshed tears. She'd hoped . . .

'You are being loyal, as a daughter should be. Even if you were adopted. But we're not enemies, Jolanda.' His hand caressed the satin of her gown. 'Not while we respond to each other in the way we do. You were prepared to sleep with me, a few days ago.' With a hypnotic stroking, his fingers were moving up to her hair and she found herself breathing heavily. 'Do you miss sex?' She felt a moist finger sweep across her mouth and realised she must have shut her eyes, flicking them open to discover that Vito's face was very close, and very, very sensual. 'Why don't we both take comfort tonight from each other?' he suggested huskily.

'I—I feel too distraught.'

She knew her face must look white with strain and hoped he wouldn't continue with his attempt to seduce her. In her present state, she felt so alone and disorientated that she might give in.

Hastily she evaded his hands and slipped off the bed, but when she turned for the door, Vito already barred the way, leaning against it and regarding her with knowing eyes.

'Then why did you come here?' he asked in a soft whisper.

His words sliced into her with their quiet menace. Startled, she searched his face. It was hard and merciless.

'I—I was frightened. Let me go back to bed, Vito.'

'You're not frightened now?'

'No.' She forced a smile. 'Only weary. Housework doesn't exactly make me feel sexy and invigorated.'

She felt as if his eyes were boring into hers, seeking the truth. She couldn't cover up her feelings well enough, and let her lids drop, staring numbly at the floor.

'Have you been spying on me?' he asked.

'Spying?' Her eyes shot up. 'To see if you have a handful of village maidens in your room? Really, Vito!'

He glanced at the table, and then back to her. Suddenly, to her relief, he smiled and moved aside, opening the door.

'I'm taking Nick to hospital tomorrow morning. The appointment has been brought forward two days,' he said. 'We'll be leaving for Taormina just before lunch. Goodbye housework, hello sexy. OK?'

Jolanda didn't trust his sudden switch of mood, nor the altered arrangements. But she'd been let off the hook, and could evade his Inquisition stare.

'Sheer heaven,' she said, as pleasantly as possible. At least she'd be safe with the prince, and maybe he could help her, if he was influential. In the morning, when Vito was away, she could try to contact her father and let him know what was going on. 'I'll go to bed now. I feel better.'

'You look it,' he said drily. 'Goodnight, Jolanda.'

Somehow she'd succeeded in deceiving him, in discovering a little more about his plans, and in avoiding his wandering hands. That was some achievement, and she ought to be delighted, she thought, when she arrived back at her own room. But her face looked woebegone and it was as if a lead weight held her down. The more she found out about Vito, the worse she felt. Dear God, it was terrible to be on such a knife-edge, keeping up appearances with him! Thank heavens he had no idea that she knew!

In his room, Vito grimly collected the documents and papers and locked them in his briefcase. Jolanda had deliberately tricked him. That could only mean one thing; she was here on behalf of her father. He knew where his duty lay. Jolanda and her father should suffer the same fate. In the candle-light, his eyes glittered. The dancing shadows sharpened his features, giving him the appearance of the devil himself.

Late into the night, he sat, ruthlessly, painfully, hardening his heart. He couldn't allow softness to interfere with his careful scheme of deceit and corruption.

*   *   *

That following afternoon, she had dressed to kill. Or, rather, to dazzle. In her favourite tight-skirted, knee-skimming white suit, her calves and ankles shown to advantage by high strappy sandals, she swayed down the stairs and out to the car. When she sat down, she deliberately leaned forwards, pretending to adjust the slender buckle on her shoe. Vito should see that she wore nothing beneath the short-sleeved jacket, whose neckline already showed a fair amount of smooth gold skin.

It puzzled her, though, when she straightened and found he looked furiously angry. The journey was a mixture of barbed insults, innuendo and long silences, and she wondered what was wrong.

They began to drive through long, long tunnels in the rock. Jolanda gripped the edge of her seat nervously. As they approached the entrance to another tunnel, she worked out from the notice by the roadway that it must be nearly two miles long. She began to shake. Ahead it looked murky and she could smell petrol fumes.

'Vito!' she croaked.

He took one look at her petrified face and accelerated, overtaking everything in sight.

'Hold on. It won't take long.'

His hand reached out and she took it, curling her fingers into the back of his hand as if he was her lifeline. The roar of the car, the darkness, the pall of exhaust, all were sending her breathing into spasm.

'A few moments more, Jolanda. I can't stop here, not on the motorway. There's a turn-off soon. Hang on. I'm here. Don't be afraid.'

'Non mi piace,' she moaned.

'No. I should have known that. Of course you don't like it.'

He was glancing at her frequently, squeezing her hand, giving her comfort by his very presence.

'*Mi dispiace,*' he said quietly.

It wasn't his fault. He had no need to apologise. '*Prego,*' she answered. '*È lontano?*'

'No. Not far. Here, ahead.'

From behind them, as they sped off the motorway, came the sound of sirens. Jolanda screamed and clapped her hands over her ears. The car screeched to a halt on the grass verge and she was in Vito's arms, every muscle screwed as tight as it could go. He pushed her head protectively against his chest so that the sound was muffled.

There was shouting outside. She felt Vito's body shift and a motion as if he was winding down the window. Everyone talked at once, Vito louder than any of them, forcibly, insistently.

'Just a minute, sweetheart,' he muttered in her ear eventually.

Jolanda felt him draw away, but his hand stayed caressingly on her shoulder. From under her spiky wet lashes, she flicked a miserable glance at the men who'd been shouting and saw a group of policemen.

'Oh, Vito! It's my fault!' she wailed, struggling to compose herself. 'Tell them! Will you be fined for speeding? Have you——?'

'Sshhh. It's OK.'

He had been searching in the pocket of his jacket, which had been laid carefully on the back seat, and produced a leather folder like a wallet, handing it to the men.

Jolanda's eyes widened. Was he bribing them? Whatever they saw, it satisfied them. They went into a huddle, presumably to extract the money, and returned the folder, smiling and waving Vito on his journey.

'Would you like to stay here for a while?' he asked quietly. 'Or find somewhere for a coffee?'

'Coffee,' she mumbled, hating the way he lived his life.

Beneath an umbrella pine, Jolanda repaired the damage to her face and felt better, sipping her thick syrupy coffee and fizzy-water chaser with pleasure now that her terrors were over.

'Why should you have known I wouldn't like the tunnels?' she asked Vito.

'Because, my darling, you're terrified of dark places. You feel trapped in them.'

'Did I get trapped somewhere when I was small?' she asked, frowning in concentration, wishing she could remember.

'Yes,' he said gently.

'You were very nice to me,' she said, placing her hand on his. 'Thank you.'

'*Prego.*'

Her frown came back again. She'd said that, in the tunnel. How odd. In her fear, she must have recalled some of the language she once knew.

Gradually she relaxed, with only the tinkle of sheeps' bells and the thin screams of swallows to disturb the awesome peace of the slumbering late afternoon. A few cows with lyre-shaped horns meandered down the road, flicking their heads to ward off flies. She smiled to see that a fanciful cowherd had wound wild flowers around their horns.

'Look,' she said warmly. 'It must be festival time around here.'

'So it must.'

Vito sounded pleased. He lifted her unresisting hand and kissed each finger slowly and thoroughly, watching her eyes all the time. She kept them lowered, knowing that he was looking for some sign of weakness towards him.

'That's heavenly,' she said, with a flirtatious smile.

His lips touched her palm and she gave an involuntary shudder.

'Why don't I find a flower meadow, where I can kiss you all over like that?' he suggested, one hand curling around the nape of her neck.

Jolanda tipped her head back and enjoyed his touch, letting her lips pout.

'Because my suit will be ruined and I won't look my best for this prince,' she laughed. 'I refuse to walk into a palace looking as if I've spent all afternoon tumbling in the hay with you.'

'Then I'd like to drive on, if you don't mind,' he said, a little tightly.

'How far is Taormina?' she asked, as he put some *lire* on the plate for the bill.

'Ask me in Italian.'

'Don't be silly!' she laughed. 'You know my knowledge of the language is minimal.'

'Well, it'll take longer on these minor roads. We won't go back on the motorway. There are dozens of tunnels yet.'

'Thank you. For a hard, embittered cynic, you can be surprisingly kind at times,' she said.

'For a shallow, brittle woman, you can be surprisingly emotional,' he retaliated, opening her door for her.

'Are we back to insults?' she said smoothly. 'Good. Let's see how many more policemen you can bribe before we hit Taormina. I do enjoy watching you pull strings.'

Vito grinned and slid into the driver's seat. 'Careful I'm not pulling yours,' he murmured.

'Hardly. I'm wise to all your tricks,' she said calmly.

'You think you're a puppet-master, and make men dance to every command of your hands? Jolanda, you have a surprise coming.'

She laughed, delighted, knowing that it was he who'd be surprised when she confronted him with her knowledge and he learned that he hadn't been successfully seducing her at all.

'I adore surprises,' she said coquettishly.

Vito's mouth quirked and his hand strayed over her thigh.

'I promise you'll get one,' he murmured.

She leaned back in her seat as they drove along the country road, letting him know that she found his caresses exciting, trying not to respond inside to them by reciting the eight times table to herself.

He was an expert in driving with one hand. His fingers wandered boldly, smoothing over the exposed skin at the back of her knee, moulding her thigh and running up higher. There his hand rested, his fingers inching further towards the place where she throbbed unremittingly. Jolanda's recitation grew muddled and hazy.

He withdrew his hand and she had to grit her teeth to stop herself blurting out a plea for him to go on, to touch her...

When she slanted a glance at him, she was shaken to see how tense he was and that the simmering anger was hardly contained. Perhaps he was annoyed that she hadn't responded by clambering all over him and demanding they stop and assuage their desire. She couldn't afford to annoy him. He might disappear the minute they arrived in Taormina, and find a willing woman. That would ruin her plans.

'Vito,' she said huskily, moving close against his shoulder and slipping a hand to caress his chest.

'Are you as hungry as I am?' he asked, in a savage undertone.

She swallowed. This was deep water. Laughter was her lifeline.

'Starving, darling,' she murmured. 'Dying to get to this oasis of civilisation and eat them dry of caviare.'

'At two thousand pounds sterling a kilo?' he mocked. 'I think you might have to do with bread and honey. What was good enough for Aphrodite ought to be good enough for you. She was given a golden honeycomb by Daedalus—you know the man who flew with his son Icarus on wings of wax? Honey is an aphrodisiac. It represents the ecstasy of love. Aphrodite installed Daedalus in her temple of Love, at Erice, in the west of the island.'

'Quaint. He sounds as if he was the original toy boy,' she commented. 'Poor man. He didn't stand a chance.'

'Sounds a marvellous fate to me,' drawled Vito. He stopped the car dead on the deserted road, and before she knew what was happening his mouth was on hers, honeyed, offering the ecstasy of love. She melted into him, her arms sliding languidly around his neck.

Then, with deliberate and steady pressure, his kiss hardened and the hands holding her grew tighter and tighter till they were steel bands. Jolanda couldn't move, could hardly breathe. He forced her mouth open and entered it with a fierce erotic kiss which shook through her body even while she grew alarmed at its intense savagery. And then he had flung her aside and driven off again.

'I can't wait for our first night in Taormina,' said Vito casually, as if he'd been shaking hands with her.

Jolanda's mouth opened and shut tightly. It was only a piece of male dominance. A little show of power and strength. She quailed at the thought of his full sexual power being unleashed on her. She must stay one step ahead of him and control the situation.

'Neither can I,' she sighed, stretching luxuriously, delighted when Vito crashed the gears and swore under his breath.

'Outskirts of Taormina,' he said grimly.

'Tell me about *Il Principe*,' she said, as they swung on to a road which climbed steadily upwards.

'Oh, he's the usual dissolute sort.'

'Sounds fascinating,' she enthused huskily.

'He is. You'll be devastated.'

'He's handsome? Youngish?'

'How eager you sound, Jolanda. I hoped we might have indulged in a little light entertainment, you and I. It sounds as though I'm to play second fiddle to a bought title.'

'Isn't he real nobility, then?' she asked. 'Doesn't he have a madly interesting family background?'

'Madly. But not noble. His father was a small-time hood. His mother was convicted of theft and his six brothers never did a day's work in their lives. Disappointed?'

'You're teasing me!' she accused. 'No one has that kind of family—oh, Vito, this place is gorgeous! Look at the views! And just look at these marvellous villas!'

'That's what I like about you, Jolanda,' he said with a faint mocking smile. 'Easily diverted. We go through here.'

He drove through a stone arch and into a narrow cobbled street, which was a mass of tumbling geraniums and plants, crowding the beautiful wrought-iron balconies.

Jolanda peered about in delight, as they bumped down alleyways, spotting some smart boutiques, antique shops, restaurants . . .

'I adore it,' she said eagerly. 'I'm going to love it here.'

'Good.' Vito was constantly slowing to avoid the parading tourists and muttering under his breath about them, driving Sicilian-style with his arm hanging outside the car to cool it. An old man waved his stick to stop the car and Vito waited with the utmost patience till he had crossed to a small café. 'We'd better stop here,' said Vito. 'I don't think we'll get any closer.'

'Aren't you going to park the car somewhere safe?' she asked in astonishment, when he stopped in the narrow street.'

'No. Someone will come for the cases and park it for us.'

'Our princeling is *that* rich?'

She felt his glance on her and slanted her eyes at him to see something like disappointment on his face. He was jealous! Jolanda laughed.

'He's influential. People do things for him.'

'Oh.' She didn't like the sound of that.

As they walked down the elegant, pedestrianised Corso Umberto, she was conscious of the looks they attracted. She supposed they made a striking couple, herself done up to the nines, and Vito strolling along with his loose-limbed, indolent strut as if he owned the place.

Though several shopkeepers did rather a lot of bowing and scraping to him, which bothered her. Was he running some kind of shady protection racket? It didn't bear thinking about.

At the end of an alley, off the Corso, a small square was bounded on three sides by wide steps, leading to a magnificent golden stone building with carved columns and arches, dark green shutters and black ironwork balconies. Jolanda's eyes sparkled. For a while she could forget Rocca and its dark, primitive way of life, and return to her usual sunny self again. Even the prospect of being sexually provocative in order to dig information out of the clam-like Vito seemed less daunting, in these surroundings.

Vito strolled with her up the steps, past huge stone pots of deep blue clematis and oleander, fan palms and jasmine. Inside it was cool and airy. Immediately, servants came to greet him, showing a great deal of respect. And to Jolanda's horror, they all addressed him in the same way.

Il Principe.

'Your face is a picture,' he drawled, thrusting his hands in his pockets and studying her mockingly.

'Yours will be all the colours of the rainbow in a few seconds,' she said in a threatening tone. 'You can't be a prince. This can't be your place. It's too grand. All that gilt and marble costs...'

Her voice died away and she bit her lip quickly, recovering her wits. Of course, if he was corrupt, he'd be making a great deal of money.

'It costs more than a man who owns a small construction company can afford,' she said a little nervously, wondering how he'd explain that one.

'Who said that was my only job?' he smiled. 'I have several. I own a vineyard, and a bottling plant, among other things. Having more than one job is a very Italian habit. I have a finger in a lot of pies.'

'Like Jack Horner in the nursery rhyme?' she asked sardonically, wanting to deflate his ego.

'No one ever told me any nursery rhymes,' he said quietly.

Jolanda felt a heel. When she and Nick were tiny, and tucked up in bed, her mother would tell them stories and teach them children's rhymes. Once or twice she'd caught sight of Vito hovering in the doorway, listening, a bleak look on his face. And despite her mother's pleas to let him stay, her father had sent Vito off to study English grammar in his bedroom alone.

'I'm sure your Sicilian mother did,' she said, in an attempt to excuse herself and her father.

'I saw very little of her in the first eighteen months of my life. After that...' His lashes swept his cheeks, hiding his eyes. 'I learned to fend for myself.'

'You've come a long way from your original back-ground,' she said softly.

'Outwardly. The rewards of a degenerate life,' he mocked, gesturing around him.

'Well, you told the truth about the prince being dis-solute. How did you come by the title?'

'By buying the palace. The two go together. Like to see your room?'

'Oh, lord,' she groaned. 'Vito, are there any other guests?'

He looked surprised. 'Now why would I invite anyone else? I wouldn't be able to seduce you with other people around.'

'Oh, darn it. I thought I was seducing you,' she said sweetly.

'For the sake of my male pride, you might pretend I'm making all the running,' he grinned.

'OK. I'll just languish whenever you deign to touch me, Highness,' she said. She erupted into giggles. '*Il Principe!* It's ridiculous! Do people really call you that?'

'Don't knock it. It gets me a load of invitations to all the best entertainments. Now, pay attention. The *palazzo* is fifteenth-century, once used by the Borgias——'

'I can feel their influence permeating the very air. I think you're one of the clever, evil Borgias, reincarnated,' she said wryly.

'—and the bed in your room is early sixteenth-century,' he continued, ignoring her. 'The tapestries here are by Pascali, your bed is by the window. The chandelier above is Venetian glass and fragile, of course, and your bed is Venetian too, but large and strong enough to house a football team——'

'I'd rather a rugby team. All those cosy, intimate scrums. Such lovely thighs,' she murmured.

'Damn! I'll have to do a bit of phoning, then,' he frowned. 'Meanwhile, observe the gold cherubs——'

'Are you trying to impress me?' she laughed.

'Am I succeeding?'

'Depends on the rugby team.'

'Here's your bedroom. Consider the bed.'

It was glorious; an ornately carved and gilded Venetian four-poster, hung with rich drapery. And it was enormous.

'I've considered,' she said calmly, walking to the window.

Delicate sheer organza, yards and yards of it, hung from a snaking, fruit-laden wooden pole. She pushed aside the material and stepped out to paradise.

'I thought here would be a good place to start,' said Vito, moving swiftly behind her stunned figure. 'And then we could move to the bed after.' His voice became husky and caressing. 'I intend to give you a night you'll never forget.'

She gave a light laugh and moved rapidly to the edge of the roof garden. Against the skyline to her right was the violet cone of Mount Etna. Below, far, far below, bordering an azure sea, were the sparkling white buildings of a beach resort, and just beneath the palace lay neat gardens, ablaze with colour and softened by shady green trees.

'That remains to be seen. However, you've given me a wonderful room,' she said, genuinely pleased.

'The bed——'

'Oh, Vito!' she laughed. 'You are incorrigible!'

'Is that good, or bad?' he asked uncertainly. Then he grinned. 'Something to eat? Or a stroll around the town? No Michael Jackson, I'm afraid, but plenty of interest otherwise.'

'Let me get out of this outfit, now I've met the prince, and into something I can walk comfortably in,' she said, going inside.

'I'll watch,' he said in a friendly tone, sitting on the bed.

'Out.'

'I get backache, peering through keyholes,' he complained, obeying. 'But I love dominant women.' He rolled his eyes.

Jolanda found herself laughing at him again, and stayed amused all the time she was changing, putting off the moment when she would have to act deceitfully. For the moment, she was enjoying herself.

They sat in a *caffè*, watching everyone pass by. Like all the men there, Vito boldly eyed all attractive women who came past, with a thorough and frank appraisal.

She did the same to the men, just to annoy him. Young lovers were everywhere, hand in hand, gazing adoringly into each other's eyes.

Vito bought her a *granita* and they drank red wine so strong that it made her bones feel weak. Across the cobbled road, a pastel artist set up his easel and began to draw a little girl. But the child was restless and bored, her face breaking into an unattractive, rubbery look of misery.

'Excuse me.'

Vito strode across to the little girl and squatted down, slightly to one side so that the artist could still see clearly. He placed his cigar in his mouth and shifted it around, catching the child's attention. He talked to her, using his eyebrows and shoulders and his restless fingers.

The child chortled and laughed. For a long time, Vito amused her, and then even his antics lost their fascination. Jolanda went over and heard the artist—apparently English—saying that he needed two more minutes and he was done.

'Come on, Vito,' she taunted. 'Can't you amuse a female for two minutes?'

He sighed, turned out his pockets, solemnly giving her their contents, and executed a neat handstand.

Jolanda put her hand over her mouth and laughed in delight as he walked around in a little circle, attracting a great deal of attention to himself.

'Finished,' said the artist.

'Thank God,' said the red-faced Vito, springing to his feet again. 'Parts of my body were beginning to go on strike, in protest.'

He accepted the thanks of the parents, admired the portrait, kissed the little girl tenderly on both cheeks and guided the grinning Jolanda back to the *caffè*.

'You are a terrible show-off,' she observed.

'Jolanda, stay in this country a few more weeks, and you'll realise that if a child cries it is the duty of everyone to rally round and amuse it. Solemn dignitaries even indulge their granddaughters by making paper airplanes out of official memos, if necessary.'

'So that's why the place seizes up; essential documents are flying around in the hands of infants. I like the Sicilian adoration of children,' she mused.

His voice lost its jaunty tone and became gentle. 'Babies and children, even in poor homes, are well dressed. Life is devoted to them. Parents will give up everything for them—and they don't grow up spoiled, either. Only brimming with self-confidence.'

'What about your parents?' she asked quietly. 'You weren't serious when you told me about *Il Principe*'s background, were you?'

His face became shuttered and dark, as though a thundercloud hovered over him.

'I described them as your father did, when we were flinging insults about,' he said morosely.

'Describe them as you knew them,' she said. 'Please. I'd like to know.'

For a moment he was silent, staring into space. 'My father was a younger brother and had defied local custom. In Sicily, family wealth depends on land. The law distributes inheritance equally. When a man dies, it is expected that the eldest son will take the land and support his own family and his brothers. The sisters will invariably marry.'

'I don't see the problem,' she said.

'If one of those brothers marries, especially if he has children, they must have a share of the land to hand down to future generations. This divides the land available until there's virtually nothing left for each one. It's normal for Sicilian brothers to forgo marriage—at least, to forgo having children. Father couldn't. He loved them too much.'

'My God!' she cried in astonishment. 'That's incredible!'

'We're very harsh with ourselves,' said Vito grimly. 'We will endure almost anything for the sake of the Family. Father existed on a small plot of land and struggled to feed his large brood. Mother was falsely accused of stealing money from the bakery and was put in prison. That's where I was born, incidentally.'

Jolanda's throat was dry. 'Was that what you meant, that time you told me you'd been in prison?' He nodded. 'Dear God! That's a terrible story, Vito.' Then she realised. In a place as small as Rocca, there would have been only one bakery. Her eyes searched his granite profile. 'Who accused your mother?' she breathed.

Slowly he turned to her, his eyes glittering, unable to hide the hate he had carried inside him for the whole of his life.

'Carlo Brabanzi,' he growled. 'Your mother's husband.'

CHAPTER EIGHT

'OH, MY God!' she muttered. 'How you must hate us all.'

He made no answer, but sipped his wine. In the silence, her mind brimming with questions, Jolanda sat unhappily, while the tourists watched the local people and the local people watched the tourists.

Life had been hostile to him. First the cold, harsh prison environment, an institution which went against all of the natural Italian exuberance and demonstrative love towards children. Then presumably back to poverty, then being orphaned, and adopted and swept away to a strange country which he hated. But why had her father bothered to adopt a ten-year-old boy who had brothers and clung to his own ways of life so fiercely? It didn't make sense. She longed to ask, but now wasn't the time.

'Shall we go back?' she asked quietly.

He nodded and they walked back without speaking until they entered the palace, where a servant met him with a message.

'It's from the clinic,' said Vito. 'The exploratory probe suggests that they can treat Nick, by removing a bone and putting him on a course of exercises.'

'Thank God!' she said fervently. 'That's marvellous news. Will this be very expensive?' she asked anxiously. The cost of all this had never occurred to her.

'Don't worry about that. I'm seeing to it. As an old friend.'

'Thank you,' she said. 'We'll find a way to repay you.'

'Perhaps.' Vito looked uncomfortable. 'They've laid supper out on the roof garden. Do you mind?' he asked.

He was so withdrawn that she didn't fear his advances. But her heart was going out to him, more and more, for every second he breathed.

She smiled faintly when she saw that they had, indeed, laid supper on the roof garden. On the ground, in fact; a dazzling white linen cloth spread with delicacies, four silver candelabra placed down the centre of it to create a romantic meal beneath the stars. And it was wasted on them.

They ate a little, drank a little, with Jolanda watching Vito all the time from under her lashes, wondering if she could ever turn him from his path of crime.

Eventually he stood up. 'I'm going to bed. Goodnight.'

'Vito...' She stopped. There was a suggestion of despair about his broad back. 'Oh, Vito!' she said, infinitely compassionate.

Slowly he turned, his face all raw bones in the hollowing candle-light.

'I need you, Jolanda,' he rasped. 'I need you!'

His voice rang across the gap between them, through the still velvet night; impassioned, shaking with emotion.

With a strangled cry, she opened her arms and he came swiftly to her, hauling her to him, bending back her body submissively beneath his.

'Jolanda, Jolanda,' he breathed. 'Heal me. Love me. Let's pretend we're in love. Don't let me spend this night alone.'

He cradled her head in his hands and kissed her with a passion born of hope and despair. Gradually that changed to something more primitive and his mouth grew more demanding, fiercer, his need for her expressed in a violent tenderness that made every inch of her body tremble in anticipation.

His hands had undone her zip before she knew and with a gasp she felt the pressure of his heated chest against her burning breast. And his hand was hotter; feverish, touching her nakedness, pushing down the resisting material of her dress over her hips, his mouth all the time devouring her as if he had seconds to live.

'No,' she whispered, then forced her voice to sound as if she meant it. 'No! Not this payment!'

'You can't refuse me,' he muttered hoarsely. 'You have no reason to.' His mouth encircled her ear, breathing heat and flames, persuasive, demanding words till her head swam. 'Pleasure all night. Here, with the warm night as a blanket, the excitement of knowing the breeze cools our skin, the feel of it on our naked bodies. You can't deny me. You've given your body to other men. Am I so different?'

'We hate each other,' she said in a slow, heavy croak.

His eyes glittered. Deliberately, he shaped his hands around the curves of her body in a rough, meaningful gesture, watching her to make sure she knew what he was telling her. The pressure of his palms and the anger in his face said it all. His hatred was total and he had to dominate her, to take her body and make it a slave to his violent passion.

'Yet we are both aroused,' he said thickly. 'Perhaps we're both jaded with bread and butter sex. Maybe we need something to revive our jaded palates, *capito*? You like being amused.' His voice became a sensual, deep growl. 'I'll amuse you as you've never been amused before, Jolanda.'

Terrified, she shrank from his blazing eyes.

'I don't think——'

'Oh, I don't want you to think at all,' he muttered, angling his dark head. 'Only...' Jolanda shuddered as his teeth grazed her shoulder '...to feel...' slid voraciously to her throat '...to hear...' ravaged the line of her jaw '...to touch... Touch me, Jolanda,' he ordered hoarsely. 'Caress my body. Feel its hardness, its urgency. Know how much I want you.'

'Vito,' she moaned, trying to stop his mouth from travelling down to her breast. She'd have no chance if—— 'Oh, God!' she gasped.

'Sweet. Nectar.' His tongue investigated. 'Growing harder.'

He was silent for a while, engrossed in an indolent, pulse-quickening slow exploration of each thrusting nipple, and Jolanda was incapable of doing or saying anything, unable to move, transfixed by the incredible pleasure she was experiencing as his mouth drew on her breast and aroused conflicting feelings within her of tenderness and pagan need.

Her head had tilted back a little, her eyes drowsy with a languor which had crept over her. Hazily she saw Vito's head lift, his lips moist, and that his eyes were focused on her parted mouth.

His face hardened and he brutally pulled up her skirt, then pressed his hands hard on her buttocks so that she was aware of the tensed muscles of his thighs and the scorching heat throbbing against her.

If she could speak, if her throat weren't filled with her choking breath, she would deny him. Only her eyes could say what she felt, and Jolanda despaired that they refused to accept the message she tried to send, which would stop him. Instead, she knew they begged and pleaded, traitorously showing him that every nerve in her body wanted him to make love to her.

'Undo my tie,' he breathed.

To her amazement, her hands drifted upwards and loosened the knot.

'Buttons.'

She swallowed and felt the fingers dig deeper into her buttocks and the slide of their hips, enticing her unbearably till she could hardly think.

'Buttons,' he repeated harshly.

Her fingers wouldn't work properly. She concentrated hard, despairing within that she was giving in to her base desires, that her body was ruling her head. But her despair was edged away, button by button, as she exposed his hard chest and its muscled curves, and her fingers strayed with pleasure over his skin, lightly touching, till between them they had shed his shirt and he slowly drew her to him so that they were just touching; each hard peak of her breast lightly rubbing against him.

Small moans erupted in her throat and she tipped her head right back, her hair falling in a wild tumble. Vito's mouth and hands raged down her body, blazing a fiery path, and then she felt the fresh night breeze around her and realised she was totally naked.

Vito hooked his foot behind her legs and they fell backwards, on to the tablecloth, his back crashing heavily on to the dishes, scattering their contents. She saw to her shock that he was oblivious to them, that he had lost all control, that he was determined to take her and nothing would stop him.

Grimly his hand removed a plate from under his shoulder and he moved a candelabra further away, his eyes like glowing coals in his head. And Jolanda was frightened, intimidated by the menace in his predatory expression, and unnerved by the triumph in his mocking mouth.

She struggled but he held her in a powerful iron grip. His knee ruthlessly parted her thighs and she wrestled with him as he effortlessly took both of her wrists in one hand and held them behind her back, slipping his fingers to her thighs and beginning to caress her with such sweet, agonising pleasure that she sobbed with it. Panting, she wriggled to avoid him, but only gave herself more illicit delight and she was mortified to hear him laugh softly.

Her head dipped and she bit him, hard.

'Little bitch,' he growled. 'You'll regret that.'

'Vito,' she snapped. 'I know you want me——'

'Oh, here it comes,' he snarled. 'Isn't this where you ask me my plans? Where you think I'm so aroused that I'll accept the offer of yourself, providing I give information in exchange? Or does your body come more expensive? Do you want me to tell the authorities to fund the site in Cornwall and so make a vast profit for you and your father?'

She stared uncomprehendingly. Vito looked suddenly haggard, the icy light of pain searing his eyes. And she looked guilty, she knew that, because she'd tried to use her sexuality to gain information.

'God, you disgust me!' he yelled, throwing her to one side.

Her body jarred into crockery but she didn't even notice.

'Vito, it isn't like that. I——'

He bent down, his hands on either side of her and looking ferocious.

'You can't have it both ways,' he grated. 'Either you genuinely want me to make love to you, or you were deliberately using your body to get what you want—as you intended with that poor European official. Which is it, Jolanda? Do I...?' He gave a grim laugh. 'No. I won't dignify it by calling it "making love". Do I have you, now, for the pure hell of it, because you want sex so badly? Taking you like a sacrificial virgin between the candles—though in your case it's a practised whore— or do you admit that you had ulterior motives in getting me aroused?'

Her whole body was tensed in every muscle. Her breathing was suspended. Whatever she said or did, she would be damned. But she couldn't let him take her in hate. He would betray her and her father, and they'd be destroyed somehow; he'd planned that all along.

'What a choice,' she whispered.

'Make it,' he said bitterly.

'You've forgotten that there might be another reason this happened,' she said, beginning to recover her wits. She sat up and tried to see where her clothes had gone. He'd thrown them in abandon in all directions. She blushed. 'I thought it would be pleasant to have you as a lover tonight,' she said. 'But you turned out to be too violent for my taste.'

With great dignity, she stood up, and collected her clothes. Vito watched her beneath glowering brows.

'You make me feel violent. You make me want to ruin that beautiful body of yours so that no man ever wants it again.'

She froze, chilled to the heart. How he did hate her.

'More threats?' She tossed her head. Standing proudly in her delicate underwear, she decided not to bother to put her dress on. She'd take a shower and wash Vito away with every drop. 'Wait till I tell my father what you've done to me. He'll half kill you. Now go. I feel dirty. I need to clean every inch of myself.'

'Bitch!' he ground out.

'Bully!' she yelled. She bent and picked up a candelabrum, waving it threateningly.

'My God, you are beautiful,' he breathed. 'Beautiful and deadly, like a poisonous snake. You deserve all you get, Jolanda. May God help you and your father. I certainly won't.'

He stormed into her bedroom and she heard the door slam violently. It was several moments before she moved. Her body gleaming in the moonlight and in the candle flames, she stood shaking, unable to believe that she had come out of the encounter in one piece.

So far.

A shudder ran through her body. Leaving the chaos on the roof garden, not even caring that the candles still burned, she ran blindly into the bedroom to lock the door and stood beneath the hot shower, her tears mingling with the fierce spray. Steeling herself, she turned on the cold tap and her body went rigid in the icy water. But it stopped her tears and soothed her puffy face. And it killed all the throbbing within her.

Roughly drying herself, she flung her damp body on to the bed and crawled between the sheets. But the shower hadn't penetrated her brain. It hadn't washed away her misery, her thoughts, her fears.

And she needed a clear head to think, not one beset with terror. Her lovely holiday in Taormina was turning out to be a nightmare.

The sky grew lighter while she wrestled with her slow brain. She must leave, of course; get to her father and pass the whole business of exposing Vito to him. God, she was tired! Her eyes would hardly keep open. With her door locked, she was safe for a while. She could sleep and then face the arduous day ahead.

*   *   *

Tossing restlessly, stifled by heat, she eventually woke to find herself hot and sticky. If her watch was right, it was nearly lunchtime! With a groan, she freshened herself up and dressed, not wasting time on make-up.

Outside she could hear a band, playing a rather miserable tune. She went to a side window and looked out. Winding its way down from the hill above was a funeral procession. Six black horses with nodding plumes drew an elaborately decorated carriage. In front was the band and behind, all swathed in black, a long, long stream of people, walking with measured tread.

Her heart thudded and her skin crawled with fear. It was a scene from her past.

'Jolanda!'

She jumped with fright at Vito's yell from the other side of her bedroom door.

'What is it?' she cried, her voice high and shaky.

'Your father's here.'

'You're lying!' she raged, wishing he were.

'Have it your own way.'

She ran to the door and put her ear to it. In the background, she could hear voices. They began to shout. And she recognised her father's bellow.

Almost weeping with relief, she unlocked the door and hurtled down the stairs into the salon, where the two men faced each other. She flung herself in her father's arms, panting.

'How did you know I needed you?' she cried. 'Thank God you've come!'

Stan Docherty fixed Vito with an expression of loathing.

'Have you hurt her? Have you harmed her?'

Jolanda drew slightly away and shot a glance at Vito. He seemed to be chiselled from ice. Even his face was white, the cheekbones standing out hard and raw.

'He hasn't hurt me,' she said quickly. 'I'm just glad to see you. I don't like it here.'

'I told you no good would come of it. This place is not your cup of tea. Neither is that bastard.'

She quailed at the hatred in her father's voice.

'Father, let's go,' she said miserably. 'We can visit Nick on the way and see how he is and——'

'*No*! Not till I've got what I came for!' yelled Stan.

'He's dangerous, Father,' she said urgently. 'Look at him! Cold and merciless! He has this island wrapped around his little finger. He even has the European Bank licking his boots because of the bribes he gives them.'

'Eh? What do you know about that?' asked Stan roughly.

'Our project in Cornwall is competing with one of his, in Rocca,' she said scornfully. 'He means to bribe officials and ensure that his pet scheme goes ahead and ours fails.'

Her father caught her shoulders and shook her in a frenzy.

'Leave her alone,' growled Vito, taking a step forwards. 'Take out your vile temper on me, as you used to. Except the difference now is that I'm a fully grown man, and you can't beat me any more. Not physically, not mentally. And not even emotionally.'

'I want my deeds,' grated Stan.

'You have what you paid for,' drawled Vito.

'*Oranges?* Crates and crates of rotting oranges?' raged Stan.

Jolanda blinked. 'What——?'

'This bastard made me pay a small fortune for a con-signment of oranges,' said her father tightly.

'That was the agreement,' said Vito, unperturbed. 'You would buy oranges. It's all on the documents. The fact that you imagined it was a customs and tax evasion, and that you were buying the dam site in Rocca, plus my construction company and the half of the company which Nick sold to me, is neither here nor there. Greed has been your downfall. You've been tricked, Docherty, and there's nothing you can do about it, since it's all legal and above board.'

'You worm!' seethed Jolanda. 'Now I suppose the way is clear for you to make a profit out of your trickery.'

'Now I tell you and your father who I am,' he said in glacial tones.

'A prince. A prince of deception, of lies, corruption and bitter revenge——'

'And an official of the European Investment Bank,' said Vito quietly.

Both Jolanda and Stan stared at him open-mouthed.

'My main job,' he said, only his eyes betraying his blistering anger and hostility. 'I investigate swindlers. Fraudulent claims, inflated estimates and developers who seem always to be involved in selling us sites at great profits. In simple terms, Jolanda, I set your father up.'

'The men at Rocca——'

'My colleagues. They knew what I was doing, of course. We've been wanting to catch your father for some time. He's the one who's corrupt and who bribes his way to success.'

'No!' she wailed. 'I won't believe you! Father——'

'I dangled the prospect of the site at Rocca in front of your father's nose, knowing he couldn't resist making another killing there,' said the implacable Vito. 'He gobbled up my business, too.'

'Another killing?' she whispered, her eyes stark.

He raked her father with icy contempt.

'Stan Docherty bought the marshy site at Rocca all those years ago when you were a child, knowing the people would have to be rehoused because of the state of the village. He falsified papers so that it appeared the site was larger and higher up the hill. He delayed construction. Not for months, but years, extracting a monthly payment from the Fund, protesting that there were expensive drainage difficulties and bribing surveyors to exaggerate the problems so he was eligible for more money.'

'You bastard. You've ruined me!' roared her father.

'You've ruined yourself. You've paid for your trickery in more ways than one,' snarled Vito, and Jolanda saw that he no longer felt it necessary to hold back. The gloves were off. Her eyes flicked between the two men in her life, utter despair choking her. 'Your payment will go nicely towards the rehousing of the people of Rocca. A sweet revenge for me.'

'The site in Cornwall——' began Stan.

'That site is unsuitable for what you proposed. The official investigating it doesn't know what he missed,' growled Vito, his eyes insolently and contemptuously touring Jolanda's body. 'We've found the men who were paid off by you to make favourable reports.' He tipped his head and, as he did so, Jolanda heard the sound of police sirens.

'You're not having my father arrested?' she asked in horror.

'Isn't that what happens to thieves?' asked Vito savagely. 'It happened to my mother and she wasn't even guilty.'

She coloured up. 'I'll tell them how you bribed the police when you were speeding——'

'I didn't bribe them. They listened to my explanation about why you were so upset in the tunnel and I showed them my identification. They understood why I had to get you to a safe place before you lost your mind. I'm trusted here. Investigators from the Bank are highly regarded. There is nothing dishonourable about the way I lead my life.'

'You've never denied the rumours of illicit deals——'

'It's my practice to deny nothing. If I have to move in criminal circles, it's useful if I'm thought one of them. Whereas I am more honest than you two in reality.'

'Not if you're mixed up in this development yourself,' she said desperately, hearing how close the sirens were. 'You want to build the dam yourself, and take the profits! With Velardi Construction and Nick's share of my company, you can! Isn't that illegal, for an official to be mixed up in something he's investigating?'

'Jolanda, you haven't been listening. Your father has bought Velardi Construction, and he is now a partner in your business too, since I sold him my share. Both are virtually worthless, of course, but he wanted a construction company to mastermind the building of the dam. He wanted it all. But he didn't reckon on the fact that I'd deliberately run my company into the ground and stripped what assets I could of yours.'

'So I'm ruined too,' she said shakily.

'It doesn't matter about you!' yelled Stan. 'What about me? A lifetime of work! Of wheeling and dealing, of holding the threads of a dozen deals... By God, Velardi! You fiddled the accounts on your company! That's falsification——'

'Terrible, isn't it?' he said in a hard tone. 'Unfortunately for you, I did it with the connivance of the Customs and Excise. The police have arrived. Do you intend to treat your daughter to a painful scene, or will you walk out into the hall of your own free will?'

'Father!' she cried piteously, clinging to him.

'For God's sake, Jolanda,' yelled Stan, pushing her away. 'Don't come to me for sympathy. I need all mine for myself. He's hit me where it hurts most. The thing I love most. My business that I was so proud of. Can't you see we're beaten?'

'We?' she whispered.

'He planned it all from the moment he knew he'd been adopted. He worked all hours, studying, forcing himself past sleep and exhaustion, intent only on revenge. You can't fight a man like that, Jolanda. He'd use any trick in the book to reach his goal.'

'But... why didn't you send him back, or——?'

'I'd lose face. More to the point, I'd lose all the advantages I gained in adopting all three of you. Business is business.'

'What do you mean, advantages?' asked Jolanda, studying her father's bitter face in a puzzled way.

'Well I didn't adopt you out of the love in my heart,' said Stan Docherty drily. 'It was Lilly's idea, not mine. But you were a pretty little thing and eager to learn. I'd have made a good businesswoman out of you, Jolanda, if this swine hadn't interfered.'

He walked out without a backward glance.

Stunned, Jolanda stood rooted to the spot. Vito had been right. Her father had meant to corrupt her, too.

The sound of the siren mingled with the thud of the monotonous drum of the funeral march, as it came closer, the rhythms resounding in her ears, making her want to scream.

She felt her breathing become shallow and rapid. Her father hadn't wanted her. He'd adopted them because of some fiddle, some... Her hands covered her face. Beyond tears, she rocked to and fro, tormented by the raucous, mournful trumpets and the dull thud of the drum as the procession entered the square in front of the palace.

'And now, you,' said Vito in his honey-menace voice.

'You've taken your revenge on me,' she whispered.

'Not where it matters most, sweetheart.'

Aghast, she lifted trembling fingers to her lips. Vito was on the point of erupting into one of his unholy rages. Unable to stand the sight of the naked lust in his eyes, she ran out of the room. But in her crazed grief, she took the wrong turning and found herself at the end of a passageway, a huge wooden door in front of her. And Vito followed behind.

She gave a wild groan and opened the door, but found herself falling down stone steps into darkness. The band was loud. She looked up to see an iron grille at street-level and feet, clad in black boots, black shoes, black stockings, marching in step.

'Jolanda! There's no light! Come out of there!' came Vito's furious voice.

He was at the top of the cellar stairs. Bruised, she shuffled on the floor away from him, terror beginning to pluck at her heart. His anger seemed to be flowing towards her as hot as lava.

And then in the darkness, in the dust and with a pain in her ribs, she remembered.

'Vito!'

He froze, chilled by the child's voice which had come from her lips. Then in a bound he was beside her, and cradling her in his arms.

Jolanda wrapped herself tightly against him and found her normal voice again.

'The clues. I understand. We were eating ice-cream, Nick and I,' she said into Vito's chest. 'A treat, because it was *feste*. There were balloons everywhere for the feast day and we'd wound wild flowers in the horns of the cattle.'

'That's right, sweetheart,' said Vito gently. 'And then?'

She shuddered and he held her tighter.

'The birds stopped singing and the water in the well began to shiver. The dogs ran for their kennels. You were at the doorway, with a message for Papa.'

'It was a challenge from my father to him,' said Vito. 'A page of insults, part of the continuing vendetta between us. You remember we weren't allowed to play together?'

'Yes. You and your family were taboo.' She drew back, the horror of what happened clear now. 'The ground shook from side to side, and then up and down! You ran over to us and shielded us with your body. Then it was dark and I was in pain and the thundering around us deafened me.'

'Have you any idea how long we were trapped by the earth and buildings?' asked Vito quietly.

'No, only that you kept talking to us and never stopped, telling us stories and raging at us when you thought we'd fallen asleep. You saved our lives. Oh, Vito! You saved me, the daughter of the man who'd denounced your mother!'

'You were a child, sweetheart. I adored you from afar. I saved you by instinct. We were buried for nearly a day and a half. Your parents, mine, my brothers and most of the villagers were killed.'

'Mamma,' she moaned. She remembered. 'She was all warm and cosy, and smelt of baking bread,' she said unhappily. 'She'd make Nicolo and me little bread men. I can't bear to think of her dying so terribly!'

'It was a terrible 'quake. Now you understand why the buildings are in such a state.'

'There were constant funerals. Long, black processions.' She looked up at him. 'People crying into black silk hankies!'

'That's right. I thought you might remember that. Actually they were strips, torn from dresses—the people were too poverty-stricken to have anything else. Ever since, I've worn a black handkerchief in my top pocket as a sign, to remind myself. As a kind of pledge.'

'A pledge.' She gulped, but couldn't hold back the swiftly flooding memories. 'We were in hospital——'

'Well, we were in temporary tents without proper facilities for a while. Stan Docherty was cruising around, seeing what profit he could make from the disaster, and Lilly found you two, starving and unwashed, in a tent, and fell in love with you. Stan saw how the hostility and mistrust of the people around melted at the sight of your mother's concern and fiddled the adoption on the spot. But there was such a media response to his "generous gesture" that he found himself adopting the boy who'd saved your lives too.'

'You didn't object then?' she asked.

'I was only semi-conscious at the time, a delayed reaction, from shock, I imagine; it happened a few days after we were rescued and airlifted out while Stan

Docherty basked in the glory,' he said wryly. 'Otherwise I wouldn't have agreed. Not to a publicity stunt. Not when it meant I was the enforced brother of my enemy's children. I'd sworn to my real father that I'd despise anyone from Carlo Brabanzi's house, for the sake of my mother's honour.'

'So you tried to make yourself unpleasant so Fath...' Jolanda bit her lip miserably. 'Oh, Vito! I'm sorry! I wish none of this had happened!'

'You've remembered. It's enough. We can't change the past. Now maybe your emotions will be unlocked. That's why I tried to jog your memory with those clues. And, I must confess, to intrigue you and divert myself. I hated to see the way you were growing colder and colder, like Stan Docherty. I knew what you were really like, underneath.'

'But why should I forget all this, when Nick remembered it?'

He shrugged. 'I don't know. You were much more tender-hearted than him. It might have hit you more deeply. It suited Stan that you thought he was your real father. He admired your strength and set about moulding it, planning that you should take over from him, knowing Nick was lost to me from the first moment we met again, when I was brought to England.'

'My father... What will become of him?'

'Nothing too severe. The charges will be concerned mainly with tax evasion. I've hit his business credibility, and that's going to hurt him enough.'

His arms left her and he stood up, looking down with the face of a man who had been through hell.

'One day, when you feel able, you must talk to Nick and learn what the people of Rocca had to go through, living in tents for four years, freezing in the bitter winters, waiting for their village to be built. Then maybe you'll understand a little better why I have been so hard on Stan Docherty. And why I was hard on you.'

'I wasn't involved with him,' she cried, springing up and catching his arm urgently. 'Not in an underhand way. I swear it! I can't bear to think how he's deceived me!'

'Oh, he had affection for you, Jolanda, out of all of us he felt warmth towards you. Anyone would. Half the men in Christendom have fought for your favours, haven't they?'

'Typical Italian exaggeration,' she said with a shaky laugh. 'The men who hoped for favours from me went away disappointed. I'm sorry,' she said again. 'Perhaps if you'd been allowed to stay in Sicily you wouldn't have grown up to avenge yourself on the world. And women in particular.'

'Women?' he frowned. 'I never gave any woman false ideas.'

'You hurt every one of my friends. By taking their virginity and——'

'My sweet Jolanda,' he drawled. 'I've made it a rule never to take a virgin. They're far too much trouble. And I certainly never touched your friends.'

'Not even the one who stripped in your office?' she asked doubtfully.

He gave a small laugh at the memory.

'I buzzed for my secretary—male—and began to dictate letters, ignoring her until she went a bright red and got dressed. Any more who bother you? The woman I brought to Sicily who had the underwear in her case searched? A fellow investigator. I'll introduce you to her and her husband and her baby son. Mandy? Ann?' He paused. 'I confess, I did that to infuriate you and to find out a little more about your business. Ann wouldn't talk, though. And Mandy got on my nerves. She had no sense of humour.'

'I'd better go home,' she said listlessly. 'There's nothing more to say, is there?'

'Home to Rocca?' he asked.

'God, no! I hate it! I'm sorry, Vito, I know it means a lot to you——'

'My sweet, I loathe the place.'

'What?'

'It has terrible memories. I was conscious throughout, listening, knowing what was happening. Every time I visit Rocca, it hurts me, deep inside, to think of the devastation and loss of life. I've been staying there for Nick's sake and to right a wrong; so the village can regain its former dignity and begin to enjoy some of the luxuries it's long been denied. But I hate it. I'm a city man. I like pavements and restaurants, opera, theatres, shows.'

He gestured with his head and she followed him up the steps, rubbing her bruised body.

'*Gesù!* I'd forgotten you'd fallen! Come, sweetheart. We'll get a doctor——'

'No need,' she said. 'I just want to lie down for a while. Then I'll leave and be out of your way.'

He watched her go up the stairs slowly, not offering to help. She'd almost hoped he would. It might give her a chance to tell him that she loved him. But he was a stubborn man, and, as he had once said, more severe with himself than any of his enemies.

Jolanda removed her clothes to check her body and put some ointment on her bruised back and ribs. Tired from the traumatic events of the day and from lack of food, she lay face down on the bed, naked, limp, feeling as if she were dead inside.

Cool hands began to stroke her back. She stiffened and then gave in to Fate, knowing those hands so well, realising it was Vito. Her pulses quickened. Perhaps she wouldn't be leaving him forever, after all.

He went into the bathroom and came back with some warm oil, trickling it on her back and gently massaging away her aches and pains—in her body and in her mind and heart. The oil was perfumed, drifting tantalising fragrances into her nostrils, of amber, musk, roses, orange-blossom... She inhaled their heady aroma and felt a deep peace.

For a long time he devoted himself to relaxing her. And then she rolled over.

'Unfair,' he husked, his facial muscles taut from control.

'You read eyes,' she said. 'Read mine.'

'I—I'm not sure I trust what I see,' he muttered. 'I think I've become illiterate suddenly.'

Jolanda laughed throatily and then she sighed.

'It's a pity you've made rules about women,' she mused, stretching her body tantalisingly.

Vito's tongue slicked over his lips.

'Rules?' he asked hoarsely.

'Mmm. About never making love to a virgin. I don't suppose you'd make an exception in my case?'

It took an agonisingly long while for the penny to drop. By that time, Jolanda had begun to undress Vito for the second time. On this occasion it was better; she knew what she was doing and spun it out, teasing him unmercifully, slapping his hand when he tried to touch her and gain the advantage.

She was just exploring his collarbone with her mouth when he murmured suddenly in her ear.

'I love you, Jolanda.'

A quiver of fire ran through her, spearing her with poignant pain.

'Love? You love me? Hard-boiled city girl who can't cook and——'

'Sweetheart, I know it's stupid and illogical and I'm a fool to fall for you, but there it is,' he said innocently.

'It's not that ridiculous,' she defended quickly. 'No more stupid than me thinking I'm in love with a devious, sneaky charmer who knows how to get his way——'

'No wonder few men have got any further than a goodnight kiss,' he muttered. 'You must have argued them into their cars before they knew what hit them.'

'And I can imagine you, slipping neatly out of women's clutches with a few well-chosen words which made them think you were respecting their honour,' she said tartly.

Vito gave a lazy grin. 'More or less,' he admitted. 'I don't think we have much option, do you? We can't be so cruel as to unleash ourselves on anyone else. Don't you think we deserve each other? I can think of nothing better than coming home to a deliciously sharp-tongued and entertaining wife.'

'I can,' she said in a sultry tone.

'I don't understand,' he said, for once his innocent look failing, to be replaced with raw animal need. And tenderness. For his hands shook as he took her fingers to his lips and kissed them. 'I don't understand,' he repeated, trying again. 'Show me what you mean.'

'You incorrigible rogue,' she whispered, showing him.

OVER THE YEARS, TELEVISION HAS BROUGHT
THE LIVES AND LOVES OF MANY CHARACTERS INTO
YOUR HOMES. NOW HARLEQUIN INTRODUCES YOU
TO THE TOWN AND PEOPLE OF

One small town—twelve terrific love stories.

GREAT READING...GREAT SAVINGS...
AND A FABULOUS FREE GIFT!

Each book set in Tyler is a self-contained love story; together, the
twelve novels stitch the fabric of the community.

By collecting proofs-of-purchase found in each Tyler book, you can
receive a fabulous gift, ABSOLUTELY FREE! And use our special
Tyler coupons to save on your next TYLER book purchase.

Join us for the fifth TYLER book,
BLAZING STAR by Suzanne Ellison, available in July.

Is there really a murder cover-up?
Will Brick and Karen overcome differences and find true love?

Harlequin Presents®

Coming Next Month

Available in July wherever paperback books are sold, or through
Harlequin Reader Service:

In the U.S.
P.O. Box 1397
Buffalo, NY
14240-1397

In Canada
P.O. Box 603
Fort Erie, Ontario
L2A 5X3

"GET AWAY FROM IT ALL" SWEEPSTAKES

HERE'S HOW THE SWEEPSTAKES WORKS

NO PURCHASE NECESSARY

To enter each drawing, complete the appropriate Official Entry Form or a 3" by 5" index card by hand-printing your name, address and phone number and the trip destination that the entry is being submitted for (i.e., Caneel Bay, Canyon Ranch or London and the English Countryside) and mailing it to: Get Away From It All Sweepstakes, P.O. Box 1397, Buffalo, New York 14269-1397.

No responsibility is assumed for lost, late or misdirected mail. Entries must be sent separately with first class postage affixed, and be received by: 4/15/92 for the Caneel Bay Vacation Drawing, 5/15/92 for the Canyon Ranch Vacation Drawing and 6/15/92 for the London and the English Countryside Vacation Drawing. Sweepstakes is open to residents of the U.S. (except Puerto Rico) and Canada, 21 years of age or older as of 5/31/92.

For complete rules send a self-addressed, stamped (WA residents need not affix return postage) envelope to: Get Away From It All Sweepstakes, P.O. Box 4892, Blair, NE 68009.

© 1992 HARLEQUIN ENTERPRISES LTD.   SWP-RLS

"GET AWAY FROM IT ALL" SWEEPSTAKES

HERE'S HOW THE SWEEPSTAKES WORKS

NO PURCHASE NECESSARY

To enter each drawing, complete the appropriate Official Entry Form or a 3" by 5" index card by hand-printing your name, address and phone number and the trip destination that the entry is being submitted for (i.e., Caneel Bay, Canyon Ranch or London and the English Countryside) and mailing it to: Get Away From It All Sweepstakes, P.O. Box 1397, Buffalo, New York 14269-1397.

No responsibility is assumed for lost, late or misdirected mail. Entries must be sent separately with first class postage affixed, and be received by: 4/15/92 for the Caneel Bay Vacation Drawing, 5/15/92 for the Canyon Ranch Vacation Drawing and 6/15/92 for the London and the English Countryside Vacation Drawing. Sweepstakes is open to residents of the U.S. (except Puerto Rico) and Canada, 21 years of age or older as of 5/31/92.

For complete rules send a self-addressed, stamped (WA residents need not affix return postage) envelope to: Get Away From It All Sweepstakes, P.O. Box 4892, Blair, NE 68009.

© 1992 HARLEQUIN ENTERPRISES LTD.   SWP-RLS

"GET AWAY FROM IT ALL"
Brand-new Subscribers-Only Sweepstakes
OFFICIAL ENTRY FORM

This entry must be received by: May 15, 1992
This month's winner will be notified by: May 31, 1992
Trip must be taken between: June 30, 1992—June 30, 1993

YES, I want to win the Canyon Ranch vacation for two. I understand the prize includes round-trip airfare and the two additional prizes revealed in the BONUS PRIZES insert.

Name _____

Address _____

City _____

State/Prov. _____ Zip/Postal Code _____

Daytime phone number _____
(Area Code)

Return entries with invoice in envelope provided. Each book in this shipment has two entry coupons — and the more coupons you enter, the better your chances of winning!
© 1992 HARLEQUIN ENTERPRISES LTD.   2M-CPN

"GET AWAY FROM IT ALL"
Brand-new Subscribers-Only Sweepstakes
OFFICIAL ENTRY FORM

This entry must be received by: May 15, 1992
This month's winner will be notified by: May 31, 1992
Trip must be taken between: June 30, 1992—June 30, 1993

YES, I want to win the Canyon Ranch vacation for two. I understand the prize includes round-trip airfare and the two additional prizes revealed in the BONUS PRIZES insert.

Name _____

Address _____

City _____

State/Prov. _____ Zip/Postal Code _____

Daytime phone number _____
(Area Code)

Return entries with invoice in envelope provided. Each book in this shipment has two entry coupons — and the more coupons you enter, the better your chances of winning!
© 1992 HARLEQUIN ENTERPRISES LTD.   2M-CPN